D0464642

Used as bait. Again.

I went flying into the office area, landed on all-fours, and slid on Fully Extended claws across an expanse of slick limoleon floor. Mellonium. It was slick, and when I stopped sliding, I found myself...

Yipes, there she stood, eight hundred pounds of Malice with horns and a fever and a grudge against the world. She had knocked over two chairs and a coffee table and scattered magazines all over the place. She had also repainted the floor. Green.

Her eyes came at me like bullets...no, like artillery shells. She was panting and volcanic smoke rolled out of her nostrils. She lowered her head, shook her horns, and pawed up a couple of magazines.

Double Trouble

John R. Erickson

Illustrations by Nicolette G. Earley
in the style of Gerald L. Holmes

Maverick Books, Inc.

MAVERICK BOOKS, INC.
Published by Maverick Books, Inc.
P.O. Box 549, Perryton, TX 79070
Phone: 806.435.7611
www.hankthecowdog.com

First published in the United States of America by Maverick Books, Inc. 2023.

1 3 5 7 9 10 8 6 4 2

Library of Congress Control Number: 2023933284

978-1-59188-179-7 (paperback); 978-1-59188-279-4 (hardcover)

Hank the Cowdog® is a registered trademark of John R. Erickson.

Printed in the United States of America

Here's another one dedicated to Kris, after 55 years of marriage. Every kid who loves Hank books should give her a hug. She was the sunlight and oxygen that made it happen.

CONTENTS

Attacked By The Charlie Air Force

It's me again, Hank the Cowdog. The mystery began on the very day it began, probably in May. Yes, it was May, and we were in the midst of the most delicious spring we'd seen in years: plenty of rain, plenty of grass, and air that was heavy with the smell of wildflowers.

I noticed the fragrance of flowers when I was jarred out of sleep by a strange voice. Wait, let's rephrase that. I wasn't asleep, couldn't have been. I'm an early-riser and it was almost ten o'clock in the morning.

Thusly, Drover might have been asleep but I was chained to my desk, as usual, doing paperwork, when I heard a mysterious voice.

"Hank, you'd better wake up. I hear an airplane."

1

I opened my…I *turned* my eyes, let us say, and saw a folks out of fracas… a frakes out of focus…a face out of focus. I could barely make out the features. The face appeared to have several eyes, at least two ears, and one nose. I had never seen the guy before.

"What do you mean, you're an airplane?"

"No, I *heard* an airplane."

"How can you be an airplane if you don't have wings?"

"No, I said…"

"Where are all the passengers? Unless you can sell some tickets, you'll go broke as an airplane."

"I *heard* an airplane!"

"Airplanes don't run in herds, cattle do. Maybe you saw some cattle. This is a cattle ranch, after all." I narrowed my eyes and took a closer loose of his lace…a closer look at his face, that is. "Who are you?"

"I'm Drover. Hi."

"I used to know a mutt named Drover. He was a lunatic."

"Yeah, it was me."

"You're a lunatic?"

"No, I'm Drover, Drover with a D."

"What is that supposed to mean, Drover with a D?"

"Well, sometimes they call me Rover but that's not me."

"You know what? I don't care. If you'll excuse me, I need to get back to work."

"You were asleep."

"How dare you say that?"

"'Cause you were and I woke you up."

I blinked my eyes and glanced around. "Where are we?"

"In our bedroom under the gas tanks."

"I thought I was in my office."

"Well, you are, but it's all the same place, under the gas tanks."

I rolled my eyes upward and saw two large fuel tanks above us. "I'm beginning to see a pattern here. We're under the gas tanks, even as we speak."

"That's what I said."

"Don't get smart with me, pal." I studied his face again, closer this time. "Wait. You're Drover, right?"

"Yeah, that's what I said."

"Why didn't you tell me you were Drover? How can I run this ranch if nobody ever tells me who they are?"

"Well, you never listen."

"Oh yeah? Well, I'm listening now, and do you know what I'm hearing?"

"An airplane?"

4

I was stunned. "How did you know that?"

"'Cause I heard it first."

"I thought you said you were herding cattle."

"No, I said…"

"If you actually heard an airplane, why didn't you turn in a report?"

"Well, I tried, but you were conked-out asleep."

I gave him a scorching glare. "Soldier, you need to get your stories straight and show some respect to your superior officers, but we'll deal with that later. Right now, we've got airplanes on the ranch. Red Alert! Form a line, load up heavy ordinance, and begin firing Anti-Aircraft Barks!"

We formed a line, rolled out the artillery, and began blasting away. We couldn't see the planes, but we could hear their motors buzzing in the distance. That was an important clue right there, the buzzing motors.

Do you see what it meant? It meant that the Charlies were using old-fashioned propeller-driven aircraft instead of modern jets, and that was good news. Those jets move so fast, it's hard to blast 'em out of the sky, even with our biggest barks.

In other words, we had a chance of inflocking some heavy damage on the Charlies, but we had to get those barks up there in the sky. So we barked and roared and blasted away with everything we had. Oh, did we bark! You should have been there to see us. It was one of the proudest moments the Security Division had seen in a long time, two brave dogs fighting off an aerial invasion of the entire Charlie Air Force.

We had been barking nonstop for several minutes when I heard a voice above the boom of our guns. "Hank, I think we're barking at the wrong thing."

I silenced my weapon and turned to the runt. "What do you mean, barking at the wrong thing?"

A silly grin slid across his chops. "What we heard was mosquitoes."

"Mosquitoes! That might be the dumbest thing you've ever said. Don't we know the difference between mosquitoes and a squadron of propeller-driven aircraft, piloted by the Charlie Air Force?"

"Listen."

"I will not listen! This is ridiculous."

"Shhh. Listen."

"Don't shush me, you little pipsqueak." I swaggered over to him and melted him with a glare. "I am in charge here and I will not..."

Suddenly I found myself, uh, listening and was astonished...you know, the little children don't need to hear this. No kidding. See, there are some parts of my work that are so sensitive, we have to slap a lock on 'em.

Here's an idea. Let's take a little break and ease the kids out of the room. Tell 'em...I don't know, tell 'em they need to brush their teeth. Don't forget how important it is for growing children to brush those teeth thirty times a day.

Is that the right number, thirty? Sounds like a lot of brushing, doesn't it? Maybe they should brush twenty times a day, but the impointant point is that we need to ease them out of the room.

Are they gone?

Okay, I guess we can move on with this, but please remember that this is **TOP SECRET** information, not to be shared or blabbed around.

Pay close attention.

Secret Bulletin #547-745

Okay, I goofed up and the kids don't need to know. Here's how it happened. Number one, we'd gotten a lot of rain that spring. Number two, when you get a lot of rain, you get a lot of wildflowers and mosquitoes, right? Number five, we like the flowers but aren't so crazy about the mosquitoes.

I mean, we hate 'em. You talk about a plague! They drill right through your hair and suck your blood, and when they're not stealing blood, they're buzzing around your ears.

That buzzness of bizzing...that business of buzzing was the most crucial piece of evidence in this case. Sometimes those mosquitoes get so big, they sound exactly like the buzz of a distant aircraft engine, the kind with a piston motor that turns the propeller.

Any dog could be fooled into thinking that he was hearing the Charlie Air Force launching a surprise morning attack on the ranch. I wasn't exactly fooled, but...hey, don't forget who turned in the first report: Drover, so don't tell me that I was fooled by the sound of buzzing mosquitoes.

I was fooled into believing that my Assistant Head of Ranch Security was something other than a goofball, and I have to take full responsibility for that. As I've said before, you can't find good help any more. These dogs today...they want a job but have no skills, and some of them are...I hate to put it this way, but some of them aren't very bright.

And don't forget that I'd been up all night, working on reports, and was mentally exhausted. When Drover turned in his bogus report, I believed him and you saw what happened next. We entered into a ridiculous conversation, then went into a Full Red Alert and wasted precious barking on a bunch of mosquitoes.

So there you have it, the hidden details behind this unfortunate incident. I'm embarrassed for the entire Security Division, and sorry we had to issue this Secret Bulletin, but I'm sure you'll agree, it was something the kids didn't need to hear. In those precious early years, they're very umprashable.

They're very impressurized.

In their early years, children tend to be very... it's maddening when I'm searching for the perfect word and can't come up with it. Children are extremely...

We can't spend all day on this. It'll come to me later on. We need to mush on with the story, so bring the kids back.

Sorry for the delay.

End of Secret Bulletin #547-745

Please Destroy!

CHAPTER TWO

The Boniness of Bones

Impressionable. There we go. Im-pres-sion-a-ble. It's one of those five-cylinder words that can get lost amidst all the deeper concepts that are flying around inside our heads. I knew I would get it sooner or later, and by George, I did.

The point is that in their precious early years, kids are very unbrushable, but they still need to brush their teeth.

Okay, back to business. Already we have the general outline of the Case of the Bogus Airplanes. First, Drover and I had been assaulted, in our own office, by a swarm of bloodthirsty mosquitoes who made so much noise, we mistook them for enemy fighter planes.

Second, we were plagued by mosquitoes because...

can you guess? The correct answer is that our ranch had experienced an unusually wet spring.

Rain = Mosquitoes.

Mosquitoes = Nuisance.

We'd love to enjoy a green ranch without mosquitoes, but it doesn't work that way. When you get one, you get the other, and even though we despised the little heathens, their annoying presence should tip you off that our ranch had finally managed to stagger out of those awful years of DROUGHT.

Had you forgotten the drought? Not me, brother. Remember *The Almost Last Roundup*? It was the almostest lastest roundup we ever had, and the reason was that our ranch had gone through three years of crushing drought. In August of Year Three, things had gotten so bad, Loper decided to round up the pastures and send every cow on the place to the sale barn.

Everybody thought the ranch was finished, and Slim even started looking for another job.

But remember what happened? Before we could get the trucks loaded, it started raining, and we're talking about raining snakes and weasels and pitchforks, buckets of rain. It rained for ten hours straight, and we ended up with five inches of water in the rain gauge.

It wrecked The Almost Last Roundup but everyone was thrilled because it broke the drought and saved the ranch. The cowboys turned the cattle out into the pasture and our lives were transfumed.

Transformed, I guess it should be. Our lives were transformed. And you know what? It kept raining! By the middle of May, we'd gotten another eight inches of rain, and most of it came slowly, which means that it soaked into the ground, just where it needed to be.

I mean, the dust clouds of depression that had hung over us for years just vanished. Suddenly, our people were smiling again. They even laughed! Grass began to grow and wildflowers popped out everywhere, acres of them, softening our world with colors and shapes we hadn't seen in years.

All at once, we found ourselves living in the middle of a flower shop that covered ten square miles. The birds came back and suddenly they were singing their little hearts out. You know me, I don't have much use for birds. They twitter and squeak all day and all night, and roost in my trees without permission, but I have to admit that it was kind of nice to have them back.

Fellers, when the birds move out, it leaves an empty space that's a little spooky. We're talking about heavy-duty, industrial-strength *silence*.

But that changed when the rains came. Now we had bugs and birds. We had made it through the drought, and it felt so good, we hardly knew how to act. I mean, after you've had a toothache for three years and it suddenly quits hurting, what do you do? What do you talk about?

We talked about the rain, that's what, and new grass and happy cows and fields of wildflowers.

But here's the other side of that soaking-into-the-ground business. I don't want to alarm anyone, but as Head of Ranch Security, it's my duty to point out that, once the ground gets soaked with moisture, any rain we get after that runs off into the draws, ravines, ditches, and creeks. In other words, a hard rain brings the danger of flash flooding and...

I'm not at liberty to say any more about this, nor can I reveal a word about the heifer that got loose in the vet's waiting room in town, so let's just drop it. Maybe it will come up again and maybe it won't, but if it does...never mind. That's all I can say.

Let's move on with the story and begin at the beginning. The beginning of a story is the very best place to begin. If you don't start there...I don't know, everything turns out crooked, I suppose, and there isn't a crooked bone in my body.

Speaking of bones, it's one of my very favorite

subjects. Do we have time to take a few questions on bones? I guess so, sure. It's a very important part of the so-forth. Ask me anything about bones. Okay, you on the back row.

"Why do dogs dig holes and bury bones?"

Great question. The main reason we bury bones should be obvious. If we didn't bury bones, if we left them exposed above ground, the cat might find them, and you know where I stand on that issue. No bones for the cat. No scraps for the cat. No nothing for the cat except trouble.

Second, bones can't dig their own holes, so we dogs have to do it for them. Who else would do it? Your average bone has no legs, paws, or claws, don't you see, while your average dog is equipped with all three.

Actually, the total comes to more than three because most dogs have four legs, four paws, and five claws on each paw.

That's a bunch of claws: 4 x 4 x 5=80.

Wait. That's impossible. I don't have eighty claws. Hmmm. Let's check the math. Okay, here's the problem. Forget the number of legs. We should have multiplied paws times claws. Check this out.

4 paws X 5 claws=20 claws.

There we go. Twenty claws come as standard

equipment on your average dog. Another question? Okay, you over there.

"A dog has FOUR claws on each paw, not five, so your math is all wrong."

Since that isn't a question, I won't dignify it with an answer. Officer, get that kid out of here! I don't have time to waste on mouthy little hoodlums. Next question? Okay, you with the big ears.

"What if a dog has only three legs?"

In the case of three-legged dogs, you have to change the equation: 3 paws x 5 claws=13 claws. Hencely, every three-legged dog has only thirteen claws, which means that he can bury 23% fewer bones than those of us with four legs, four paws, and twenty claws.

But even three-legged dogs are glad to help a bone now and then. It's something a dog can do for a bone that a bone can't do for itself, and every bone needs a friend.

Is this awesome or what? I get a kick out of these press conferences.

Any more questions about bones? Okay, you in the middle.

"Which kind of bone is bonier: chicken bones, beef bones or ham bones?"

Another great question. It's a fascinating subject, the boniness of bones, and I've done a lot of research on it. Our studies suggest that there is a broad level of boniness in all bones, but some bones are bonier than others. Furthermore, a beef bone will never be a ham bone, and neither will ever turn up in a chicken.

To make matters even more complicated, turkeys have bones too. We call them "turkey bones," and for some reason, they appear on the ranch around Thanksgiving and Christmas. We're not sure why, but they do.

Another question on bones? Okay, you on the front row.

"Do you have a position on ham hocks?"

Absolutely, yes. Every dog in America should have an opportunity to eat a ham hock. They're great! In one little package, we get several nice bones, a few bites of ham, and several wads of pork fat, all enclosed in a chewy wrapper of pig skin.

On this outfit, Sally May cooks her turnip greens and pinto beans with ham hocks, and bless her heart, she gives them to us dogs. Why? Because she doesn't want her family eating them. Too much fat. Good, what a deal! I love 'em.

That business about them being too fat is nonsense. Any dog that can't handle the fat in a ham hock...okay, there was that one time when the fat content ran a little high and I'll admit that it gave me a touch of indigestion. I had to do Reruns and it really grossed her out. Sally May, that is. It grosses her out when I do reruns.

How was I supposed to know that she was watching? I mean, she'd gone back inside the house. I guess I should have known she'd be spying through the kitchen window. The woman sees everything around here, especially awkward events that involve me. I think she has radar.

Anyway, she saw the whole thing and screeched something about me being the most repulsive dog she'd ever known. It really hurt my feelings. I try SO HARD to please her. Oh well.

How did we get on the subject of ham hocks? I thought we were talking about rainfall and flowers. Hmmm. That's kind of a big jump.

Never mind. We're out of time for questions anyway. Don't forget, I'm a very busy dog with a lot more on his plate than ham hocks.

Tell you what, let's start all over from scratch, and that brings to mind another concern: scratching.

Have you noticed that the flea population has exploded since we started getting all this moisture? It has. They're everywhere and our Scratching Activity has gone off the charts. Since the middle of March, scratching has increased three hundred percent. How can I run this ranch if I'm scratching all the time?

Anyway, where were we? I have no idea.

Does anyone remember what we were talking about?

Phooey.

Let's change chapters and try to get organized.

Wet Boots

Oh yes. Drover had heard some mosquitoes buzzing and turned in a bogus Red Alert about enemy bombers. That sounds crazy, but it's the kind of thing I have to live with every day.

Now we're cooking.

I left the office, took the elevator down to the first floor, and went looking for some new scenery and fresh air. As you might expect, Drover went back to bed and probably dreamed about airplanes.

I hiked up to the machine shed and checked out the Ford hubcap that serves as our dog bowl. Sniff, sniff. It contained chunks of material that we call "Co-op Dog Food." It had the texture of gravel, the smell of stale grease, and the taste of sawdust.

No dog with a shred of pride would eat such

slop, but we do it every day. I mean, what's the alternative? It's cither eat the stuff or shrivel down to bones and sinews, so we swallow our pride and swallow the Co-op.

Crunch, crunch.

See what I mean? Rocks made of petrified sawdust. One of these days, all my teeth will break off and what will our people think about having a toothless dog in charge of the Security Division? That won't be funny and it will serve them right.

Crunch, crunch.

On the other hand, once you've gotten over the shock of breaking rocks with your teeth, it's not as bad as you thought it might be. Sometimes it's a little difficult to flush the particles down the pipe, but then you notice a glimmer of taste lingering on your taste bulbs, and you realize that stale grease is better than no grease at all.

Actually, it's pretty good if you're not expecting steak, and you'll never hear me complaining about the food on this ranch. Your poodles and your town dogs would squall for days if they had to eat Co-op, but out here, we consider it good honest American dog food, the ration for Dogs Who Keep The Country Running.

Anyway, I was in the mist of these thoughts when I heard footsteps approaching from the

west. I turned and saw that the footsteps were caused by Slim Chance's boots thumping on the ground. In other words, Slim was approaching and he was wearing boots.

He walked up to me and gave me a pleasant look. "Morning, pooch."

Six months ago, before we started getting rain and green grass, his face would have looked like a piece of beef jerky—dried up, wrinkled, and hard. He wouldn't have been smiling and he sure wouldn't have spoken to me in a pleasant tone of voice.

Hey, he even reached down and scratched me behind the ears, and you know how important that is to a dog. Even tough guys involved in Security Work love to have our ears scratched, so I cranked up the tail section and wagged out a greeting.

He pointed to...well, to his boots, it seemed. "Lookie here, pooch." They were an old pair of Red Wing lace-ups that had never been polished in their entire lives. "They're wet."

Our eyes met and I went to Slow Puzzled Wags. Okay, his boots were wet. Was there more to this?

His grin grew wider. "That's from dew on the grass and weeds. When was the last time anyone on this outfit got his boots wet, walking around headquarters? It means this old ground is soaked up with moisture, and I'm so proud of my wet boots, I might even burst into song. What do you think? You want to hear my wet boots song?"

My tail froze in the Neutral position. I didn't want to discourage the guy or tromp on his creativity, but in all honesty, no, I did NOT want to hear another of his corny songs, especially one about wet boots.

I mean, of all the weird things to sing about! Wet boots? Who would think of composing such a song, and what kind of dog would want to listen to it?

No one. Not one dog in the entire state of Texas would want to listen to a song about his wet boots.

Sigh.

We dogs go to great lengths to support our cowboys. We want them to be safe and happy. We want them to be successful in all the silly things they do. We don't want to be disrespectful or insensitive, but I *did not* want to hear his song.

I delivered this message through Sad Eyes and Tail Wags. It sailed past him like a dove in a high wind.

He pulled up a five-gallon bucket, sat down in front of me, and sang his song. There was no chance that I could escape. I had to listen to every word and every note. You want to hear it?

Wet Boots

Wet boots, wet boots
Bring shouts and hoots
Of happiness, boy, this is dandy!
We've come through the drought,
Depression and doubt,
I'd rather have wet boots than candy.

Now pooch, you remember how droughty it got,
Three years we spent in that jail.
Month after month, we just couldn't buy
Enough rain to put rust on a nail.

The grass withered up, the ground it was bare,
The elm trees were dying in droves.
Even the cedars, the toughest of trees,
Rolled over and turned up their toes.

Wet boots, wet boots
Bring shouts and hoots
Of happiness, boy, this is dandy!
We've come through the drought,
Depression and doubt,
I'd rather have wet boots than candy.

For thirty-six months we looked to the sky
And waited for something to fall.
What fell was the market for cattle and beef.
No rain, snow or drizzle at all.

Now look at this place, you'd think it was Ireland!
The lamb's quarter's grown five foot tall.
My boot leather's soaked up the dew like a sponge.
And fellers, I'm having a ball!

　Wet boots, wet boots
　Bring shouts and hoots
　Of happiness, boy, this is dandy!
　We've come through the drought,
　Depression and doubt,
　I'd rather have wet boots than...
　Fried chicken, cherry pie, ice cream, or donuts,
　I'd rather have wet boots than candy.

He finished the song and turned a big grin in my direction. "What do you think? You know, a big shot called me from Nashville the other night, wanted me to appear at the Grand Old Opry and sing that very song in front of thousands of people. I told 'im no, I had too much work out here and couldn't stand the thought of being away from my dogs. Was that the right decision?"

I studied his face and switched the tail over to Slow Taps. Let's be honest. There are times when I'm not sure whether to believe him or not. Did he actually get a call from Hashville, or was this some kind of garbage report he was putting out for his dog?

He's said this kind of thing before, you know, about people calling him, and the thing I've noticed is that when he talks about it, a kind of flicker comes into his eyes, and he bites one side of his lower lip. Does that mean anything?

Maybe not. Okay, he'd asked for my opinion, so here goes. I hadn't expected much from a song called "Wet Boots." I mean, right away you know it's not going to be a love song, right? But I'd heard him sing worse and, actually, it was kind of neat, the way he used his wet boots as a way of expressing the droughtness of a drought.

Not bad, and I could see that he was proud of it, so I limbered up the tail section and gave him Wags of Applause. I even barked because, well, a dog needs to encourage his people, and if a little bark can brighten their day, I'm glad to do it.

Again, he scratched me behind the ears. "Hank, you're about three bales short of a full load, but, boy, you've got good taste in music."

I wasn't sure exactly how to respond to that,

but it didn't matter. Just then, and I mean at that very moment, we heard a voice calling Slim's name. It was a woman's voice, and since we don't have many women on this outfit, I was pretty sure that it had come from Sally May, the boss's wife.

We both looked toward the house, and sure enough, she was standing at the yard gate, and she called out again.

"Slim? Telephone call for you."

Slim frowned. "Who'd be calling me?"

I wondered about that too. Hey, wait! Maybe it was the guy from Hashville, and get this, maybe he would send us a whole box of CANNED HASH.

Well, why not? Hashville is famous for its hash, right? Maybe you didn't think of that, but it's obvious when you do the math. Check this out:

Hash + Ville = Hashville. Or we can turn it around and do it the other way: Hashville – Ville = Hash.

Wow, is this cool or what? But here's the best part. Maybe Slim would share the hash with his best friend in the whole world, his loyal dog, the guy who listened to his corny song about wet boots. Here, check this out:

Hash + Can Opener + Dog = Happy Dog.

I had a feeling this was going to be a good day. Slim pushed himself up from the bucket and shuffled down to the house. Naturally, I followed. That's what loyal dogs do, we follow our people. I had no idea what I would find at the yard gate, and neither do you, but it wasn't hash. I'm not going to give you any hints about the cat, so you'd better keep reading.

CHAPTER FOUR

Toad Patrol

T hree surprises awaited me when I reached the yard gate. First, Drover was there. Perhaps he had fallen out of bed. Second, he was playing with a toad.

Two surprises, actually. Two surprises were waiting for me at the gate, and they were both surprising.

Slim went into the house and I marched over to Drover. "What are you doing?"

"Oh, hi. I found a frog."

"You found a *toad*. That's a toad, not a frog."

"Yeah, but they're the same thing."

"They're similar but not the same. See, toads belong to a branch of the animal kingdom called 'aquariums.' That group includes other creatures that live part-time in water, such as your salmonellas, your turtles, and your so-forths."

"I think they're *amphibians*, not aquariums."

This caught me off guard. "You've got a point. 'Aquarium' is the branch of the animal family that incudes fish. Fish are aquariums, toads are amphillibans, and what you've found there is a toad."

"Yeah, and we haven't seen any toads in ages."

"That's correct. Do you know why?"

"Well, let me think." He rolled his eyes up to the sky. "They fly south in the winter?"

"No. Toads don't fly south. They don't even fly north, because toads don't fly. They have no wings."

"Oh yeah. They hop."

"Exactly, but during periods of drought, they quit hopping and disappear. This one has returned, due to all the rain we've gotten. Rain makes them hop."

"I'll be derned. Where do they go during the drought?"

"They burrow into the mud."

"How can they find mud in a drought?"

"I don't communicate with toads. I don't know."

"A lot of times, you see 'em smashed on the road."

"Excellent point. In a wet spring, they come out of the mud, hop on the roads, and get squashed by passing vehicles."

"Yeah, a toad on the road, and that rhymes."

"Exactly. They become bloody little pancakes of toady material."

"Boy, I love pancakes."

"Yes, but Sally May seldom shares them with her dogs."

"Speaking of roads, beavers are road-dents."

I gazed into his eyes and saw...well, almost nothing. "What did you say?"

"They've got buck teeth."

"Pancakes have buck teeth?"

"No, beavers do, 'cause they're rodents, and they chew trees."

"Oh, I see. You're partly right. Beavers chew trees, but they do it with *beaver* teeth, not buck teeth. Only buck deers have buck teeth."

"What about ducks?"

"Ducks have *duck* teeth, not buck teeth."

"What about duck tape?"

"Ducks have duck tape, of course, and without duck tape, the average ranch would crumble."

"Yeah, that's what cookies do."

"What?"

"Cookies crumble. I wish I had one."

"Yes, and so do I." There was a long moment of silence. "Drover, how did we get on the subject of cookies?"

"I'm not sure."

"Hmm. Perhaps we hopped from one subject to another."

At that moment, the toad hopped and Drover let out a squeak. "Oh yeah, the toad! Let's chase him!"

"Great idea."

I added my barks to Drover's squeaks, and to our delight, every time we barked or squeaked, the toad hopped and we followed him with our noses. Wow, you talk about something that will bring excitement into your day! We were completely absorbed in this good wholesome entertainment, when I happened to glance around and saw...the cat. Mister Never Sweat. Pete.

He was sitting on the other side of the fence with his tail wrapped around his bottom-side. He was staring at us with his weird yellow eyes, and smirking. That's Pete, always smirking.

In his usual whiny voice, he said, "Well, well! It's Hankie the Wonder Dog, with his comical sidekick!"

Most of the time, our best response to a cat is to ignore him and go on about our business. Cats hate to be ignored, don't you know, and whatever a cat hates is high on my list of things to do.

So I ignored him, I mean, didn't even give him a look or a nod. The toad hopped and Drover and I stayed right on him with our noses to the ground. I had completely shut kitty out of my mind but he kept running his mouth.

"My, my, our dogs are chasing a frog! How meaningful!"

Did I have time to get pulled into a confrontation with the cat? No, but there was something in his tone of voice that I couldn't ignore. Remember the Motto of the Security Division? *Do unto others, but don't take trash off the cats.* We ignore the kitties as long as we can, but when they start talking trash, we respond with sirens and lights.

I lumbered over to the fence. "That isn't a frog."

"But Hankie, it hops."

"So do kangaroos and they're not frogs either. That is a *toad.* If you're going to flap your big mouth, at least get the terms right."

"My goodness, Hankie, I had no idea you were so fussy about details."

"Hey, Pete, in Security Work, we deal with the Real World and we have to get the details right. If you don't want to be part of the Real World, go someplace else."

"I wouldn't know where to go."

"Exactly, so play by the rules. Oh, when you said that Drover and I were engaged in a 'meaningful' activity, I noted a tone of mockery in your voice."

His jaw dropped. "You mean it showed? I had no idea."

I had to laugh. "Everything shows when you're dealing with the Security Division, right Drover?" I whipped my gaze around and caught him staring off into space.

"Oh, hi. Did you say something?"

"I'm interrogating the cat. Maybe you'd like to pay attention."

"Oh, sorry. I was thinking about cookies."

"Stop thinking about cookies." Back to the cat. "You were mocking us, Kitty. I picked it up in your insolent tone. You might as well admit it."

He heaved a sigh. "Very well, Hankie. When you're around, there's no place to hide."

"Exactly right."

"I admit that, watching the two of you, so intent on..." He snorted a laugh. "...so intent on chasing a toad, I was swept away by the thought…"

"Hurry up."

"Sorry. I was swept away by the thought… *these dogs look so ridiculous!*" He broke into a spasm of cheap, irreverent laughter.

I whirled around to Drover. This time he'd been listening. "Did you hear that?"

"Yeah, but he must have been talking about someone else."

"He was talking about us."

"Yeah, but…we didn't look ridiculous, did we?"

"Of course not. We were doing our jobs. If we don't check out the toads, who's going to do it?"

"Yeah, but Pete's still grinning."

We studied the little sneak. "That's more than a grin. It's a smirk."

Drover began to sniffle. "Yeah, and it really hurts my feelings. All my life, I've wanted to look unridiculous. All we did was chase a toad!"

He began to cry and I laid a paw on his shoulder. "Be brave, son, there might be a solution to this."

He sniffled and wiped his eyes. "You think so?"

"Yes. Why don't you jump into the yard and beat the snot out of him?"

His eyes grew wide. "Me?"

"Of course. You were the one most deeply wounded by his mockery."

"Yeah, but this old leg…what if he fights back?"

"Cats are pure bluff. Give 'em a show of force and they'll run."

For a long moment, he gazed at the cat, and I could see an expression of steel forming in his eyes. "You know what? I think I can do this."

"Of course you can."

"When you take all you can take off a cat, you can't take any more."

"I couldn't have said it better."

"He needs to pay for this!"

Before my very eyes, he jumped the fence… okay, it wasn't quite that dramatic. He tried to jump the fence but ended up scratching and clawing his way into the yard. But by George, he got there.

I was surprised. Where had this fire come from? He'd spent his whole life being a little chicken, yet now he'd been swept up in some kind of…I don't know, passion or moral outrage, I suppose. Maybe he'd finally reached his breaking point.

I watched as he marched straight toward the insolent cat. Boy, I was proud! Two feet away, he stopped, faced the cat, and began shoveling up grass with his front paws.

Then, in a firm term of vone, he said…this is a direct quote…he said, "Okay, Pete, you're going to get it now!"

Kitty gave him a sultry glance. "I beg your pardon?"

"You're really going to get it this time. I've had it up to here!"

"Oh really?"

I held my breath and waited for things to blow sky high, but we've got to change chapters. Don't go anywhere. You'll want to find out what happened.

Is this exciting or what?

CHAPTER FIVE

Drover's Big Fight With The Cat

Okay, there we were. Drover had launched a Special Ops mission into the yard. His objective was to beat the snot out of the local cat. I held my breath, waiting for the explosions to start going off. I mean, the tension in the air was so thick, you could have cut it with hot butter.

Drover shifted into his fighting crouch. He was glaring at the cat and shoveling grass with his left front paw. Wow.

Over the years, I had tried to school the little mutt and give him a few pointers on fighting. We had covered the whole nine yards of combat: kajudo, karotto, boxing, glaring, snarling, hurling insults, pawing up dirt, and all the rest.

But, to be real honest, I thought he'd slept

through the lessons, and I sure never expected to see anything like THIS. But there he was, my worst pupil, the bottom of the class, a guy I'd thought was a dunce—there he was, pawing up dirt and growling like a two thousand-pound bull!

Amazing. You know, those of us who devote our lives to the teaching profession go through days when we think, "They're so dumb, why bother?" I mean, we look into the eyes of a student and see a two-hole latrine. I know that sounds cruel, but it's true.

But what I was seeing in the yard brought a rush of joy and pride to my weary heart. I even cheered him on. "Go get 'im, son, and don't forget the left jab!"

He loosened up the neck muscles in his neck. "I'm on it. He's fixing to get a big fat lip!" He leaped out of his corner and danced toward the center of the ring, shooting out jabs and glaring deadly glares at the cat.

Pete...well, he didn't do much of anything, except smirk and flick the last two inches of his insolent little tail. Right then, I knew that Kitty had come into this fight out of shape and over-confident. He hadn't done his roadwork or spent any time training in the gym, which meant that he was completely estum-underrating the rage that was smoldering inside my fighter's heart.

Drover lowered his chin and moved forward like....I don't know, like some kind of wrecking machine on four legs. Now he was within range for his jab and...

I couldn't believe this. The cat broke out LAUGHING. We're talking about hysterical, insane laughter. He left the center of the ring and staggered back to the iris patch, cackling like a flock of crows.

Drover was stunned, I mean, his eyes looked like full moons. His gloves dropped to his sides, he gave me a helpless look, and croaked, "He didn't do anything!"

"Well, you were supposed to beat the snot out of him."

"Yeah, but..." He was so confused, he fell to the ground and began kicking all four legs, and bawling.

Oh brother. Now what? The Security Division's contender in the

Shrimp Division had laid down and thrown the match, and our worst enemy was laughing his head off. Unless someone took charge of events and turned this deal around, the entire Security Division was going to be buried under the most humiliating defeat in our history.

I had been pacing outside the yard and it became clear that pacing wasn't going to help. Something had to be done about this outrage. I grabbed a big gulp of air, leaped over the fence in one graceful bound, and marched over to the little chicken-liver who had brought us to the brink of humiliation.

"Get on your feet! We'll tag-team the little crook."

He stared at me through tear-drenched eyes. "What?"

"I'll take the first shift and soften him up, then you hit him with everything you've got. Do you copy?"

He struggled to his feet. "Got it. Roger that. I'm really mad now."

"You're mad, but are you determined in your heart?"

"Oh yeah, my heart's completely undermined!"

"Good. Let's go get him!"

I cruised across the yard like a battleship, loading the big guns as I moved toward the iris patch. Somehow it never occurred to me to glance back over my shoulder to make sure the other ships in the task force were backing me up. I had only one thing on my mind: getting revenge on the cat.

The little scrounge made no attempt to conceal his location, I mean, the iris patch was throbbing with his laughter. Good. Before I got done, he would be throbbing with something a whole lot worse.

I gave him no warning, just dived straight into...

Never mind. Let's skip this. Don't forget, there are some parts of my work that I can't share with the public.

Do you really want to know that this world we call Home is filled with cheaters who cheat all the time? And who corrupt the atmosphere for the rest of us?

That's a terrible lesson to be passing along and it just breaks my heart.

Sigh.

Oh well, we might as well get this over with.

Okay, everybody knows that cats are notorious liars and cheaters, right? You bet. They would rather cheat and tell lies than eat breakfast, and they're especially adept at using a certain trick called The Rake.

Here's how it works. Instead of coming out and fighting man-to-man, dog-to-dog, or cat-to-cat, they will leap onto the back of an opponent, settle into a position on the neckolary region, and proceed to rake the opponent's lips, nose, ears, cheeks, and gums with a blizzard of claws.

It's against the rules, against the law, against the very notion of fair play and common decency, but they do it anyway. Do you know why? BECAUSE CATS LOVE TO CHEAT. BECAUSE CATS...

Listen, once you've got a screeching cat on the back of your neck, it's hard to shuck him off, and you wouldn't believe how much damage a sniveling little cat can do with twenty sharp claws. It's shocking.

I guess you've figured it out by now. The little crook leaped on the back of my neck and was in the process of raking big chunks of skin and tissue off my face, when, all at once, the back door burst open and out stepped the Lady of the House. Sally May.

I guess she'd heard the uproar. Yes, we'd been making quite an uproar.

Right away, she noticed that...well, the brawl had spilled into her flowerbed and the posies had taken a pounding. Was that my fault? No, but guess who got blamed.

"Hank, leave the cat alone and get out of my flower bed!"

Leave the cat alone? Hey, I would have been

glad to leave the stupid cat alone, but I was wearing him like a bonnet of razor blades, and he seemed pretty serious about tearing off my ears.

Do you remember that little pile of caliche rocks that Sally May keeps on the back porch? On an ordinary day, she's got five or six of them stashed near the door. She chunks them at cottontail rabbits that sneak into her yard and graze on her flowers.

She's been known to chunk them at dogs too. She's got a good throwing arm and has a wicked fastball. She's more accurate than you might suppose, and those rocks really hurt.

She bent over, snatched up a rock, drew her back her arm, and let it fly. Everything I knew about Sally May made me think that she had ME in mind as the target, but this time she beaned the cat. Right on his fat bohunkus!

Reeeeer! Hiss!

Tee hee! I loved it. Great shot!

Her mouth dropped open. "Oh Pete, I'm sorry! I was trying..."

The cat jumped straight up in the air. When he came back to Earth, I began warming up Engines One and Two, and Sally May must have, well, read my thoughts. She does that quite often, you know.

"Hank! Don't you dare!"

See what I mean? She has bugged our phones and hacked into all our systems. She's got Radar For Naughty Thoughts. We have no privacy on this ranch and no dog is safe around that woman.

Okay, maybe my intentions had been pretty obvious. I'm a very honest dog, you know, and I've never been good at concealing my thoughts, and my thoughts right then were pretty muchly concentrated on hamburgerizing her rotten little cat. And perhaps she noticed.

Of course she noticed. She sees EVERYTHING.

She came down the porch steps like...like I don't know what, but the way she marched told it all: mouth and eyes pinched, stiff arms swinging, heavy tromps on the feet. It spelled Trouble.

My head and tail sank. She towered over me. "Leave the cat alone! What's wrong with you? And look what you've done to my flowers!"

Well, it appeared that our relationship had suffered another setback and I felt terrible about it. My tail switched into Automatic and began tapping out a mournful rhythm.

It was then that I noticed...well, she was wearing a pair of rubber sandals, those things with a piece of rubber that fits into the fork of two toes. They're call "slip-slops," and sometimes she

47

wears them around the house.

Flip-flops is what they're called. Flip-flops.

But the impointant point is that she wore no socks. Her feet and ankles were bare and suddenly it came to me in a flash, a plan for patching up our relationship.

You'll never guess what it was.

CHAPTER SIX

Bad Idea

Let's be honest. Over the years, my relationship with Sally May had suffered more than its share of ups and downs, and I can't tell you how much sadness it had brought into my life. Hey, not just sadness. Torment.

I worry about it day and night. Sometimes I'm not able to sleep, no kidding. I mean, what does it take to please her and become The Dog of Her Dreams?

I know what you're thinking: "Stay out of her yard and leave the cat alone." Everyone rushes to the Simple Answer, right? We all yearn for Life to be plain and simple, but it doesn't always work that way.

If Life was really that simple, why did we keep

repeating the same cycles, over and over again? I mean, I knew all this stuff, but here I was again, in her yard and in trouble for wanting to wreck her rotten little cat.

I just don't get it, and my heart aches when Sally May and I find ourselves in these awkward moments, when she's flinging rocks and screeching at me, and I'm being devoured by guilt and self-rebeek.

Self-*rebuke*, I guess it should be, when I'm being devoured by all the whatevers.

It cuts the heart right out of the Dogness of a dog. We're supposed to be loyal and true. We're supposed to please our people, make them happy and bring sunshine into their lives. But then everything falls apart and we find ourselves engulfed in anger, insults, and misunderstandings, and quivering under the terrible lash of guilt.

It makes a dog want to give up and quit trying.

But remember those flip-flops? Her feet and ankles were bare, right? What if...what if I *licked her on the ankles*? I mean, what other gesture could capture the, the, the...the remorseness of my remorse, the sorrowness of my sorrow, the guiltiness of my guilt, and express my burning desire to patch things up once and for all?

I had to try it! I mean, things had gotten about as bad as they could get and we needed to

pump new life into our relationship.

I moistened up my tongue, leaned forward, and delivered three loving, juicy licks on her...

"Aaaaaaaa!"

Oops.

She snatched her foot away and set me ablaze with her eyes. "Don't lick me on the ankles! You know I hate that!"

I knew that? Hey, a dog can't remember everything.

She bent at the waist and roasted me with her glare. "I know where that tongue has been and I don't want it on my feet! Now scat, get out of my yard!"

Fine. I could take a hint. I tucked my tail between my legs and was about to slink out of her life, when the door burst open and out stepped Slim and Loper.

Their faces showed concern. Loper glanced around the yard and said, "We heard someone scream."

"It wasn't 'someone.' It was your wife."

"Is everything okay?"

"No, everything is NOT okay." She thrust a finger in my direction, I mean, like a spear. "Him! Your dog."

The guys seemed relieved and shared a grin, then Slim said to Loper, "Thanks for the use of the phone."

"You sure you don't need my help?"

"I can handle it. When you've got good help, you don't need much of it." He gave Loper a wink.

I had been trying to listen to this conversation, but for some reason, my gaze kept going back... well, it kept going back to Sally May's feet in the flick-flocks, and to the bare flesh of her ankles. They were such pretty ankles and...

Maybe my technique had been wrong the first time. Maybe my tongue had been too wet with love and devotion. That can happen, you know.

Hey, it just didn't make any sense that she'd

reacted in such a weird manner. A woman should understand the deep emotional so-forth behind a good Ankle Wash, right? I mean, you wouldn't expect a clod like Slim to appreciate it, but women? They're more in touch with their feelings, see, and maybe if I cut down on the water...

I had to give it another try. I just couldn't bear the thought of leaving our relationship in such terrible shape. If there was any hope of patching things up, I had to walk the extra mile.

"Aaaaaa!"

Gee, you'd have thought she stepped on a scorpion.

Her eyes flamed at me. "Will you stop licking my feet? Slim, please get this dog out of my yard!"

Slim shook his head and opened the yard gate. "Come on, Prince Charming, I think you've wore out your welcome."

As I slank through the gate, she speared me with another gaze. "That is the most...oh!"

As I've said before, a dog's most difficult task in this life is trying to figure out what it takes to be a Good Dog, and sometimes we fail. We must move on with our lives and mush on with the mush.

Loper had been watching and listening and laughing. "Hon, Hank loves you."

She searched the yard for some ammo, found a

small stick, and threw it at him. Laughing, he ducked back into the house.

Oh, by the way, as I was slinking out of her precious yard, my ears picked up the sound of gleeful snickers coming from the iris patch. I turned my eyes to the east and saw a grinning face, peeking through the iris plants. THE CAT.

He would pay for this!

I followed Slim out the gate and we headed toward the machine shed. I could feel his gaze prowling around on the top of my head and knew he was about to make a smart remark, and of course he did.

"Hank, you sure have a way with the women."

See? What did I tell you?

"I believe you could start a fire in wet grass. It's a real gift."

Make one little mistake around here and they hang it around your neck forever.

"I've had my share of flops, but buddy, that was the Flop of the Month. You make me look like Arnold Flynn."

Sometimes I have to ignore him. I mean, the guy just raves on and on.

But since he brought up my Flop of the Month, let me point out a tiny detail that a lot of dogs would have missed. Did you happen to notice that my "flop" had occurred while a certain lady was wearing **flip-flop** sandals?

Was that a clue that might explain her weird behavior? Maybe not. Never mind.

When we reached the machine shed, I noticed Drover's head peeking out the crack between the big sliding doors. Good. We could get started on his court martial and put him in jail where he belonged.

But then I noticed something else. His head hung upon his neck like a limp rag and his eyes seemed to have been hollowed out by some kind of... well, tragedy. He looked sad, defeated. I slowed my pace and studied the little mutt, and before I knew it, the steam had gone out of my anger.

I walked over to him. "What's wrong with you?"

He sniffled. "How'd you know something was wrong?"

"I have eyes. You look awful."

"Yeah, 'cause I feel awful."

"Welcome to the club. So do I."

"Well, I feel awfuler than you do."

"That's impossible. How awful do you feel?"

"Twenty-five."

"I feel twenty-eight."

"I guess you win."

"What are you feeling so bad about?"

He sniffled. "Pete laughed at me. He made

fun of my stub tail!"

"He didn't say a word about your tail."

"Yeah, but he said I looked ridiculous, and I know what he meant. Everyone makes fun of my tail. I hate my tail!"

I took a deep breath. "Drover, he said we both looked ridiculous, because we were chasing a toad."

His gaze slid in my direction. "You really think that was it?"

"Of course. And you know what? He had a point. Viewed from a certain angle, two dogs chasing a toad might be considered ridiculous."

A little smile peeked through the fog of his mog. "I hadn't thought of that. So maybe my tail isn't as bad as I thought?"

"Your tail is fine. Maybe it's a little...it's fine, Drover, stop fretting."

The little smile grew and bloomed all over his face. He came skipping out of the machine shed and sat down beside me. "Thanks, Hank, I feel better now. But you don't look so good."

"Because I feel lousy, I mean crushed. I tried so hard to please Sally May, but it blew up in my face."

"Yeah, I saw."

"You did?"

He bobbed his head. "You want some advice?"

"No, I do not want advice from a chicken-hearted, stub-tailed little hypocardiac."

He collapsed and started bawling. "There it is, my tail again! I knew it! You hate my tail!"

"Okay, I'm sorry, I take it back. You have a great tail."

"You're just saying that."

"No, I'm sincere."

His eye peeked out from behind a paw. "Promise on your Cowdog Oath?"

"On my Cowdog Oats, I promise that you have a great little tail."

He wiped his eyes and sat up. "Well, if you're being sincere, that means a lot. You want some advice?"

"No, I do not want..." There was as long, tense moment of silence. "Okay, I'll accept one small piece of advice."

He leaned toward me and whispered, "Don't lick her on the ankles. She hates it."

Reactivated For Special Duty

His words hit me like a wooden nickel. I flinched. "How was I supposed to know that she hates being licked on the ankles?"

"'Cause every time you do it, she blows a gasket, but you keep doing it."

"You mean...wait. Are you saying that I don't listen? Is that your point?"

"Yep."

I rose to my feet, paced away from him, and gazed off into the distance. My mind was churning. "I hadn't considered that. So you're saying that if I stop licking her on the ankles..." I paced back to him. "Drover, you must promise me one thing."

"Oh sure, anything."

"You must promise on your Cowdog Oath *never* to tell anyone that I listened to your advice. If word of this ever leaked out, it would be very bad for the morale of our unit. I'm sure you understand."

"Oh sure."

"Promise you won't tell?"

He raised his right paw. "On my Cowdog Oats."

I laid my paw on his shoulder. "Soldier, I think we've made some real progress. This day got off to a bad start, but now it's time for us to get on with our lives."

Pretty touching, huh? You bet. The clouds of gloom had blown away and we had worked through some heavy business. Drover had grown more comfortable with his Inner Tail, and I had been forced to confront a very difficult concept, that our Beloved Ranch Wife didn't want me licking her ankles. Not only did she not want it, she hated it.

Wow. It had been quite a session.

I'm sure you noticed that I told Drover a small fib about his tail and concealed it by swearing on my Cowdog *Oats* instead of my Cowdog Oath. Was that clever or what? See, an Oath has to be the truth, straight down the line, but when you swear on your Oats, you can get by with stretching the truth a little bit.

I did it for his own good, don't you see. It was not only clever but compassionate as well. He had a ridiculous tail, but there was no point in dwelling on it.

Oh, by the way, we had to postpone Drover's court martial, because right then, Slim came out of the machine shed and walked toward the pickup. That could mean only one thing: he would soon climb inside, start the engine, and drive off to some new adventure on the ranch.

My ears leaped up and my gaze locked on him like a laser bean. I waited for him to activate our unit. I mean, if he had work to do, he would need dogs to help, right? That meant us, the Elite Troops of the Security Division.

I waited, my ears in the Alert Position and my legs trembling. See, when they call us up, we like to respond in a crisp, professional manner: sprint to the pickup and leap into the cab with wild abandon. That seemed especially important today, after my dismal experience with Sally May and her pampered little cat.

I waited and watched and quivered. He climbed into the cab, started the motor, let out on the clutch, and...I couldn't believe it...he drove away! Without us!

I was shattered. "Well, it's happened. We've

been deactivated."

"Oh, goodie."

"What?"

"I said...oh rats. What'll we do?"

"I guess we'll get on with your court martial."

"Me? Gosh, what did I do?"

"The list of charges is so long, I hardly know where to begin, but let's get started."

"He stopped."

"No, I said let's *start*. Once we start, we can't stop."

"No, I said Slim stopped."

I turned my Visual Scanners toward the east and picked up an important clue: Slim had stopped. "It doesn't matter. The court martial will..."

I heard a tiny wisp of sound and turned back to Drover. He was gone, had vanished into thin air, leaving nothing but a few dog hairs and flakes of dandruff floating in the breeze.

"Drover? Return to base at once, and that is a direct order! Drover?"

The pickup horn honked and Slim's voice pierced the silence. "Hank, come on, let's go!"

Holy smokes, I'd gotten fresh orders, I'd been reactivated!

I rammed the throttle up to Turbo Five and went roaring toward the pickup. Slim was holding the door open, so I Raised Gear and went flying into the cab, crashed against the passenger-side door, whirled around, leaped into his lap, and licked his cheek and ear five times before he pushed me away.

"Quit!"

He slipped the gear-shift lever into first and we chugged away from headquarters. I rushed to the open window and stuck my nose outside, drinking in gulps of delicious spring air. I had no idea where we were going, and it didn't matter.

I was back in the saddle, back on the job! Oh, happy day! Drover? He had vanished, but his time would come.

We drove north to the mailbox and turned east on the county road. About two miles east, we came to Slim's mailbox and I thought we might turn there, but we kept going. At the low-water crossing, Slim had to slow down because water was running across the road.

When we reached the middle of the crossing, the back tires began to slip and spin. He reached down and pulled the transfer case lever into four-wheel drive, and said, "Moss."

Moss? What was that supposed to mean?

"Moss grows on the concrete, makes it slick."

Oh.

"If we didn't have four-wheel drive, we'd be sitting in the middle of the creek, spinning our tires."

Oh. Well, good thing we had four-wheel drive.

We crossed the creek and continued down the road. We rumbled over a cattle guard and were no longer on our ranch.

Hmm. I began to wonder where we were going and what sort of mission this was going to be. Maybe Slim noticed my curiosity (with these cowboys, we're never sure what they notice), and he spoke.

"That was Viola on the phone. She and her daddy need some help."

Yes? And?

"They've got a heifer with an infection. Woodrow wants to haul her to the vet, and that got me to thinking. We've got a high-dollar cowdog on the ranch and we might as well put him to work."

Who? Oh, me? Sure, no problem. One heifer, one cowdog, one job done right. That's the way we do business around here.

He was watching me out of the corner of his eye. "You know, pooch, sometimes the boss looks at his dog food bill and wonders what he's getting for thirty bucks a month."

I stiffened and gave him a glare. For thirty

bucks a month, he was getting the complete Ranch Security Package, which included Special Crimes, Early Warning, Traffic, Tire Wash, Chicken House slurp...Chicken House Patrol, The Sharing of Pain, and Babysitting.

THAT WAS A LOT. That was Full Coverage, the biggest bargain in Texas.

And since he had brought up this tiresome subject, could we talk about the quality of our local dog food? Loper bought *the cheapest brand on the market*—not the one with the most taste or the best texture, but the cheapest.

It came in fifty-pound sacks like sand-mix cement, and it tasted about the same. It was probably cheaper than sand-mix cement, which was the only reason he fed us Co-op instead of cement.

Don't get me started on this, and don't talk to me about the dog food bill.

I didn't mean to get so stirred up, but I get sick of them yelping and moaning about the dog food bill.

But you know what? I don't think he understood one word of it. It went right past his ear like a bat on the porch at night.

"Viola said the heifer might be a little snuffy."

Snuffy?

"And might want to harm someone."

Harm someone?

"That's why I brung you, Hankie."

Oh yeah? Maybe we needed to talk about that.

"I mean, you're so big and strong and brave, quick, fast on your feet, an incredible athlete."

Well, yes, that was true. Good point.

"And perceptive."

Another great point.

"If things get out of hand, we might need to use you as bait."

I stared at him. Bait! What was that supposed to mean?

A grin spread across his face. "You make the best cow bait of any dog I've ever been around, pooch."

I heaved a weary sigh and looked out the window. Okay, this was another of his pathetic attempts at humor. We dogs not only have to put up with his corny songs and his griping about the dog food bill, we have sit in a moving pickup and listen to his stale jokes. I mean, the guy thinks he's a comedian or something, and he's not even close.

Who but a dog would put up with this stuff? Not a wife, not a cat, not even a goat. You know what? Slim didn't deserve a loyal dog. No, by George, he deserved a wolverine that would bite a hunk out of his toe every time started flapping his mouth and trying to be funny.

Sorry, I didn't mean to get carried away, but sometimes I get tired of trying to play Mister Nice Doggie. I'm not as nice as they think.

Anyway, where were we? I don't remember. Oh yes, the cat. Pete had really sand-bagged me on that deal, but we weren't talking about the cat. We were on our way to Viola's house to load a heifer that thought she was hot stuff, and I would have to send her to school and convince her that she wasn't.

That would be a piece of cake, and best of all, I would be performing in front of a lady who absolutely adored me. See, Miss Viola might have been engaged to Slim, but don't let anyone fool you. She was crazy about ME. In fact, that probably explained why I had been called out on his mission—because Viola was lonely and wanted to see me again.

Good. I was on my way.

A Sick Heifer

We pulled up in front of the old two-story house where Miss Viola lived with her aging parents. It had a nice porch that went around three sides of the house and a glider swing on the front, big enough to hold two people. In fact, I had been present on several occasions when Slim and Viola had sat in that very swing, sometimes talking and sometimes playing their instruments.

Slim got out and glanced around. Seeing nobody, he leaned into the open window and spoke to me. "I'll check things out. You stay here and try not to embarrass me with any more of your weird behavior."

Weird behavior. Oh brother.

I waited until I heard the squeak of the gate

hinges before I dived out the window. Maybe you thought Slim had told me to stay in the pickup, but that's not the way I understood it. He'd said, "Stay here," which meant "stay on the ranch," not "stay in the pickup."

Communication is very important in my line of work. We not only have to interpret their words, but also what they mean. It's pretty tough sometimes. Half the time, they mumble their words and the other half, they're pulling some kind of childish prank on the dogs.

But here's the point. Slim probably wanted me to check out the location of Viola's two dogs, Black and Jack.

You might have missed this important detail. See, those mutts hadn't met us at the cattle guard or barked us all the way to the house, something they always did, no matter the weather or time of day. Something was going on around here and I felt sure that, in his deepest heart, Slim wanted me to check it out.

Anyway, he went to the house and I dived out the window, confident that he would approve of my mission, checking out the local mutts. They were loud, overbearing, and obnoxious, and it struck me as kind of mysterious they hadn't intercepted us when we arrived.

It didn't take me long to solve the mystery. Heh. Someone had locked them in a dog kennel behind the house, and there they sat, staring out at the world and wearing long, sad faces. I could see that they needed some cheering up.

"Morning, boys."

Black swept me with a sour gaze and muttered, "Oh great."

Jack made teeth at me and added his two cents' worth. "Shove off."

"Thanks. I can't stay long, just wanted to drop by and say howdy. We missed you at the cattle guard."

They glared at me and said nothing.

"Gosh, I guess they locked you up. What's the deal?"

They traded glances, and Black said, "Do we have to listen to his big mouth?"

"Yeah. We're snookered."

"I ain't sure I can stand it."

"We've got no choice."

I walked in front of them and studied their kennel, six feet of cyclone fencing attached to steel posts set in cement. "Boy, they fixed you a nice place here. A six-foot fence! Does that make it hard for y'all to jump out?"

"Listen, jerk, if we ever get out of here, you'll be scrambled eggs."

I smiled. "I know, but not today. Listen, don't worry about watering those trees over there. I'll give 'em a few squirts. I know you guys are busy."

Black's eyes smoldered. Jack's eyes crackled like the flash from a welder, and he growled, "Stay away from our trees!"

I waved goodbye. "You boys have a great day."

Hee hee. Boy, you talk about loving your job! This was great. On my way back to the pickup, I had just enough time to do a Quick Squirt on those trees before leaping back into the cab.

When Slim returned, I was sitting in the seat, a statue of Perfect Innocence, and he never suspected a thing. Hee hee.

"Come on, pooch, we've got work to do."

Yes sir! I leaped out the window and fell in step beside him. As we were walking toward the corrals, Rosella, Viola's mother, came out on the porch and yelled, "Slim, make sure Woodrow is wearing his hat, else he's liable to get sunstroke!"

"Yes ma'am."

We continued our hike down to the corrals and found Viola and her dad, looking across the fence at an eight-hundred pound heifer with horns.

Woodrow was wearing his usual set of clothes: a blue denim work shirt and khaki pants that bagged in the seat, held up by a pair of red suspenders. And no hat.

He was talking to Viola and seemed irritated. "I can load the darned heifer by myself! You didn't need to call that boyfriend of yours."

Viola sighed. "His name is Slim."

"I know his name."

"He's not just my boyfriend. We're engaged."

"I know that too and I don't need his help."

She saw us, smiled and waved. "Here he is right now!"

"Well, it took him long enough to get here."

Viola came toward us, lighting up the whole world with her smile. She gave Slim a hug and rubbed me on the ears. Slim walked over to Woodrow, whose white hair fluttered in the breeze.

Slim offered his hand and they shook. Woodrow growled, "I told her not to bother you."

"It's no bother. I'm glad to help."

"She wasted your time. This won't take five minutes."

"I'm supposed to tell you to wear your hat."

Woodrow glared at him. "I wouldn't wear that thing to a dog fight on a dark night." He bent over and picked up a kind of helmet, brown, with a wide brim all around. "She found it at a garage sale. It makes me look like Jungle Jim."

Viola tried to bite back a smile. "Daddy, it

protects your ears from the sun."

Woodrow pitched it on the ground. "I'd rather not have ears. That's the silliest thing I ever saw."

Viola glanced at Slim and rolled her eyes.

Woodrow pointed toward the heifer. "There she is. We had to pull her calf and it was dead. I don't think she's cleaned out and she's got an infection. I could have loaded her myself."

The heifer stared at us with listless eyes and seemed harmless enough. It was pretty obvious that she didn't feel good.

Woodrow had already hooked up a sixteen-foot bumper-hitch stock trailer to his pickup and had backed it up to the loading chute. Slim studied the layout of the pens and checked to be sure all the gates were set.

"Well, this ought to be easy enough."

"That's what I told this stubborn girl, but she don't listen."

Slim walked into the pen. "Come on, pooch, let's get her loaded."

We walked toward the heifer. Sometimes sick animals will fight, don't you know, but this one... well, she took one look at ME and that was enough. She trotted down the alley and hopped into the trailer.

Slim closed the gate and that was it, a textbook

example of cow-loading. Everything worked so slick, I didn't even have to bark.

Woodrow and Viola came along behind. Viola said, "Daddy, do you want me and Slim to take her to town?"

"No! I can still drive." He breezed past Slim. "Thanks."

The old gentleman climbed into the pickup, started the motor, and was all set to head for town when...this was a little hard to believe but I saw it myself...the heifer made a leap upward, straddled the top of trailer gate, tumbled out, landed on the ground, and headed right back to the pen where she'd come from.

Slim said, "Good honk!" He ran to the pickup and stopped Woodrow before he drove off . "Hey, she jumped out."

"Who jumped out?"

"Your heifer."

Woodrow shut off the motor and we went back into the corrals to study the situation. It was obvious that something had changed. The heifer didn't look so friendly now. She was glaring at us, swishing her tail, and shoveling dirt with a front foot.

Woodrow shook his head. "Well, you've got her stirred up now."

"Daddy, nobody got her stirred up. She jumped

out because she wanted to jump out."

"She's not used to strangers."

Viola gave him a sweet smile. "All right. We'll leave and you can load her yourself."

Woodrow flinched. "Don't get your nose out of joint."

"Do you want help or not?"

Woodrow turned to Slim. "See what you can do and try not to chouse her around."

Slim chuckled. "Ten-four, but what if she tries to chouse me around?"

"Well, I don't care, as long as you don't get her hot and stirred up."

Slim stepped into the pen and walked toward the heifer. She should have turned and trotted into the alley. She didn't. She shoveled dirt, lowered her head, and made a razoo at Slim. He bailed over the fence just as she slammed into it.

I, uh, changed my location and moved behind Viola's legs, just in case the old rip had any big ideas.

"Hank?" It was Slim, of course. His gaze found me as I was, well, peeking around Viola's legs. I went to Slow Wags on the tail. "Hank, it's time for Plan B. See what you can do."

Me? Hey, that heifer was ready to fight! Could we...

Oh brother.

CHAPTER NINE

I Load the Heifer, Pretty Amazing

It always happens this way, you know. They wait until the situation is hopeless, then they send in the dog. Great. Well, it had to be done and the good part was that I would have an opportunity to show off in front of Miss Viola.

Did I mention that she was crazy about me? She was. I mean, she liked Slim too, don't get me wrong, and that's why she wore his engagement ring on the third toe of her left front paw.

The third finger of her left hand, I guess it should be.

Maybe you remember that ring. Slim bought it with his cowboy wages and it had a microscopic diamond in the middle. He bought it to replace the lock washer he'd given her the day he proposed to her in front of his saddle shed.

I was there and saw the whole thing. You talk about shocked! Slim Chance, Mister Bachelor America, engaged? I was speechless.

Even so, there remained a special magic between me and Viola. She not only liked dogs in general, but she was especially fond of me and recognized all my better qualities: dashing good looks, great personality, awesome nose, drop-dead good looks, enormous shoulders, charming eyes, physical courage, bold tail, and dashing good looks.

We don't have time to go through the entire list, but this gives you an idea of why she was nuts about me. Slim was a nice guy and, in theory, he was her financee, but don't let anyone fool you, the lady was over-the-moon crazy about ME.

Hmm. What were we discussing? I seem to have lost the thread of my needle. Something about the moon? Maybe that was it.

Wait, skip the moon. We were talking about the heifer, and I was fixing to load her all by myself, while the lovely Miss Viola watched and cheered me on to victory. Slim wouldn't appreciate me showing my stuff in front of his girlfriend, but that couldn't be helped.

It was Show Time. I gave Viola one last adoring glance, slipped under the bottom board of the corral fence, and entered the pen in which the heifer was standing in which. I swaggered up to her.

"Okay, ma'am, I understand that you're sick and in a bad mood, but you have an appointment with the vet. Do a left-face, head for the gate, and let's get this over with."

She stared at me like a chunk of wood, so I switched to the next phase of the procedure, leaned forward and directed my daggerish gaze right into her eyes. Then I put icing on the turnips and delivered one loud, crisp bark. Surely that would...

Most of the time, that's all it takes, one good crisp bark on top of the daggerish glare, but, well, she was too dumb to figure it out, and don't forget, she wasn't normal. She had a fever and had been acting waspy.

So I wasn't the least bit surprised when she... okay, I was pretty surprised when she came at me like a train, an irrational, ill-tempered train with murder on her mind. Who could have predicted that? Nobody. And her ambush-out-of-nowhere caught me half a step behind.

Do we need to go into details here? No. But I will say this. Your waspy types of cattle have a cheap trick they use on dogs, whereupon they scoop up the dog with their horns and fling their heads in an upward direction. There are a lot of big muscles in a cow's neck, don't you see, and...

We're talking about airborne. Flying lessons. I landed right in front of Miss Viola, who screamed, burst into tears, and cried, "Oh, Hank! Beloved, heroic Hank, hast thou been wounded beyond all repair?"

Okay, those weren't her exact words and she didn't exactly burst into tears, but she was concerned. Don't forget, she adored me.

By now, the heifer was banging her head against the fence and it was pretty clear that she had no intention of going anywhere. Slim pulled on his chin and sized up the situation. "Woodrow, how bad do you want that heifer to go to town?"

Woodrow was a little hard of hearing. "Say what?"

Slim raised his voice and tried again. "How bad do you want that heifer to go to town?"

"Well, she's sick and needs help."

"That's all I need to know. You go to the house and have a cup of coffee. We'll load the heifer and haul her to town."

Woodrow's shaggy eyebrows pressed down on his eyes, and he turned to Viola. "What's he up to?" She shrugged. Woodrow turned back to Slim. "I can haul my own darned cattle."

Slim shifted the toothpick to the other side of his mouth and said nothing.

The old gentleman seemed at a loss for words, then he did something that I thought was pretty strange. He leaned down and patted me on the head. "Doggie, you're the only one around here who's got any sense." He glared at Slim. "I'm going to the house for coffee." And with that, he left.

Viola was biting back a smile. "Well done! Now what?"

Slim gave her a wink. "I'll be right back." And he left.

Wow, all at once, I found myself alone with the sweetest, prettiest lady in the whole state of Texas! Hey, maybe Slim would...I don't know, maybe he would just vanish and Viola and I could run away to a castle in the mountains and live happy ever-afterly.

Minutes passed and we heard the sound of a motor. It seemed to be coming from inside the barn. A moment later, we saw a tractor coming our way, and guess who was driving. Slim.

Viola cocked her head to the side. "What in the world is he doing?"

Neither of us had any idea why he had brought the tractor, but we soon found out. He pulled up to the corral and gestured for Viola to open the gate. She did and he drove the tractor into the pen with the heifer, who also seemed puzzled.

Do you see what was going on here? Ha! What a great idea! You know, these cowboys come up with a lot of bonehead ideas and they spend entirely too much time pulling pranks on their dogs, but this time, old Slim had used his head.

See, that tractor had a hydraulic front-end loader with a scoop. He headed toward the heifer. She swished her tail, pawed up some dirt, and charged the scoop. Bam! Slim lowered the scoop, picked her up, lifted her three feet in the air, and dumped her out.

That was all the old hag needed to know about tractors. She headed for the gate and trotted down the alley, with Slim right behind her in the tractor. When she came to the trailer gate, she changed her mind, whirled around, and charged the scoop again, but Slim convinced her that she really wanted to jump into the trailer.

Viola was standing by with the trailer gate and latched it shut, then beamed a smile at Slim and said, "You're such a hero!"

That might have been an exaggeration, but I had to give the old boy credit. His Plan C had worked a whole lot better than...although I should add an important detail. See, Slim did a pretty good job with the tractor, but I followed along behind in the Cleanup Position and fired off some amazing barks, just in case the heifer needed more persuading.

And by George, it worked! Between me and Slim and the tractor, we parked her in the trailer where she belonged, and just in case she had ideas about jumping out again, Slim got a catch-rope, pitched a loop around her horns, and tied her to the trailer.

Pretty slick, huh? Like I said, I could have done it by myself, but I was glad Slim was around to make his little contribution.

Now, all we had to do was haul her to town and drop her off at the vet clinic. No big deal, right?

CHAPTER TEN

I Have To Share the Lady With Slim

After I had gotten the ill-tempered heifer where she belonged, I noticed that Slim's gaze had turned up to the sky, where big puffy Gulf clouds were drifting from east to west. "Radio said we have a good chance of rain this evening and those clouds have a stormy look."

Viola slipped her hand into the crook of his arm and they walked toward the pickup. When he opened the door, I was, well, coiled and ready to spring into action.

He gave me a hard look. "Did someone dial your number?"

My number? Not exactly, but I was pretty sure that Viola wanted me to ride up front in the cab.

"You sure flunked your heifer test."

Well, I...it was complicated, but we got her loaded, right?

"Get in and try to act halfway civilized."

Oh yes, I could handle that. Halfway civilized was no big deal for me. Hey, in the presence of a lady, I could push it up to sixty percent. I sprang into the cab and took my spot next to the shotgun-side window.

We pulled away from the pens and passed in front of the house. Woodrow was standing on the porch, holding a cup of coffee and watching us. He didn't wave goodbye but raised his cup.

Viola said, "He appreciated your help."

Slim laughed. "What ever gave you that idea?"

"Well, I know him. He's too proud to say it, but he was glad you came. I predict he'll even mail you a check."

"He don't need to pay me anything."

Up to that moment, I had been listening to their conversation, but all at once, it occurred to me that...well, Slim was getting a WHOLE LOT of attention from Viola, and I was getting zilch.

You know me, I don't mind sharing once in a while, but for crying out loud, the guy was hogging my lady friend. Okay, maybe I was feeling a tiny sting of jealousy, but bear in mind that I'm just a dog, not a saint, and normal dogs experience jealous feelings once in a while.

Hencely, I slithered across Viola's lap and more or less inserted my awesome body into the space between them. They needed some adult supervision, right?

She continued the conversation. "Of course he should pay you! Your time and knowledge are worth something. If he had tried to load that heifer by himself, he might have ended up in the emergency room. It would have cost a ton of money and think of the poor nurses. You deserve to be paid."

Slim chuckled. "Well, don't tell him I loaded her with the tractor. He'll cut my wages in half."

She still wasn't paying attention to me, I mean, I could have been a sack of groceries or a watermelon sitting on the seat. Something needed to be done about this. I had no intention of letting it continue all the way to town.

I rose to my feet, gave her a gallant cowdog smile, and licked her on the cheek. I did this expecting... well, some kind of warmth or kindness. I mean, she was one of the sweetest ladies I'd ever known.

Furthermore, she not only loved me, she loved me TEN TIMES MORE than she loved Slim, and who could be surprised at that? Slim had his good points, but in an honest contest with me, he had no chance. I was better looking and twice as charming and had a heart of purist gold.

Also, and this is important, my living room wasn't decorated with dirty socks, and I didn't live on a diet of boiled turkey necks and mackerel sandwiches. I mean, the guy was ODD.

So I licked her on the cheek, in hopes of coaxing her back into the corral of my attention span, and was really surprised when she, well, pitched me across the seat and against the passenger-side door.

And then—this was the killer—and then she scooted over next to the skinny bachelor and continued STARING at him with dreamy eyes!

Shocked, is what I was, not only that she had dismissed me in such a rude manner, but that she had done it so easily. Hey, I'm no poodle, I'm a big guy, and tossing me across the seat had been no ball of wax.

These ranch gals will fool you. They might put on lipstick and eye paint, but they can also lift a bale of hay and know how to give a dog the heave-ho. I guess the point here is...well, don't mess with the girls when they're in the middle of a conversation.

I knew that. It had just slipped my mind.

Anyway, my heart broke into a hundred and

twenty-three pieces and shattered like a fragile wine gomlet...omlet...globule...like a fragile globlet...broke like a fragile...phooey.

My heart *broke*, is the point, and my hopes sank. She scooted over next to the oaf and continued staring at him with dreamy eyes.

"Daddy has been in the cattle business all his life, but he's never loaded a fighting cow with a tractor. I don't know anyone who has. It was so clever, so inventive! How did you ever think of that?"

Slim grinned and his face turned a shade of pink. "Well, fear had a lot to do with it, and a long history of getting wrecked by cows. When stupid don't work time after time, a guy begins to use his mind."

"You have such a way with words!" Her gaze went past Slim and out the window. "Oh my, look at those wildflowers!"

Slim slowed down and looked out at the pasture, an unending tapestry of red, yellow, orange, and blue flowers, folded into swirls of little white daisies.

Slim nodded. "Yeah, it's amazing what rain will do. But you know what? They're just weeds."

"That's what Daddy says."

"Well, it's true. Cows won't eat most of 'em."

She gave him a hard look. "Slim, sometimes what cows don't eat is what makes life worthwhile. It's called 'Beauty.'"

"Yes ma'am."

She heaved a sigh and rolled her eyes upward. "Slim, you *must stop* calling me 'ma'am.' I'm not just a rancher's daughter down the creek. We're engaged."

"Yes ma'am."

She set her jaw and drilled him in the ribs with a knuckle. He yelped and laughed and almost ran off the road.

Well, this seemed a good time for me to reload, regroup, and relaunch my campaign to bring her thoughts back where they belonged, to ME. Creeping toward her inch by inch, I crept toward her inch by inch, until, hey what a deal, I found myself sitting in her lap!

They were still laughing and not paying attention (good), so I continued my snakely slither across her lap and poured my enormous body into the space between them. There, I switched all circuits into a program we call Quiet As a Mouse. I held my breath and waited. Would they notice?

At last their laughter faded and her gaze drifted down and landed on me. "How did you get back here?"

Me? I didn't recall ever leaving. I'd been there for hours.

She pinched her face into a funny expression that was about half-mad and half-amused. "Hank, you're such a scamp. I want to sit next to Slim."

Why? What about me?

She pointed to the space on her right side. "You can sit over here and snuggle all you want, but you can't sit between us."

Slim growled, "Hank, move!"

Gee, how can a dog express his deepest emulsions if they don't let him...fine, I could move. I slank across her lap like a sad refugee, with tucked tail, deflated ears, and eyes whose candle had been snuffed out by a cold, cruel wind.

Once I had crossed her lap and reached the Far Side of Human Warmth, she scooted closer to Whatshisname and laid her head upon his shoulder. This was so sad, I almost wept. I had been cast aside like an old shoe.

I could have given up right there, just surrendered to the so-forths of the so-forth, but I'm no quitter. Those of us who climb tall mountains don't stop and whimper because there's more mountain to climb. No sir. We catch our breath, swallow the bitter taste, and keep truckin'.

And so it was that while the lovely Miss Viola leaned her head on Slim's shoulder, I leaned my head on her right arm, and even applied pressure with my legs, so as to squeeze out every inch of space between us.

Slim had to continue driving, of course, and after a while I heard him grumble, "Y'all are about to push me out the door."

Tough toenails. By George, I owned one side of her and had no intention of slacking off.

Heh heh. As I've said before, the mind of a dog is an awesome thing.

When we rolled into Twitchell, Viola said, "Do we have time to stop at the Dixie Dog and get a cherry lime?"

Slim was checking the clouds. They were

clumping together and rolling up into big gray mountains in the sky.

"It's looking stormy. We'd better unload the heifer and get back home. I don't want Woodrow coming after me with his shotgun."

He turned right at the stoplight and drove to the vet clinic on the east edge of town. There, he backed the trailer up to the loading chute and went inside to find Dr. Skaggs. Viola went with him, and what was I supposed to do, sit in the cab and count the flies? No sir, I bailed out the window.

Doc was inside, spraying the cement floor with a water hose. This was the enclosed area where he worked on cattle and horses. He wore scuffed boots and a plaid short-sleeved western shirt. I had done business with him before (snakebite) and...

I might as well be honest. I tried to bite him. I mean, what's a dog supposed to do when they slip up behind you with a hypodeemic nurdle? A hypodermic needle, I guess it should be, and he looked like some kind of vampire. Even so, I had to admit that he was a nice fellow, gentle and patient, and I was sorry that I had tried to bite him.

He turned off the hose and Slim told him about the heifer. "Woodrow thinks she's got an infection. She also has an attitude problem."

Viola had been listening. "Slim loaded her in

the trailer with a tractor."

Doc gave Slim a long look. "John Wayne would have used a horse, the Cowboy Way."

"Yeah, well, John was busy today."

Doc nodded. "Bring her in and I'll catch her in the chute."

"Be quick with the head gate."

"Slim, I've done this before."

"I'm just telling you, don't fall asleep at the switch."

Doc took a deep breath and walked over to the west wall, where he tapped his finger on a framed piece of paper. "Do you own one of these?"

Slim moved closer and squinted. "Texas A&M School of Veggitary Medicine."

"Veterinary Medicine. It's a doctor's degree. You don't get one unless you can operate a head gate."

"Boy, you sure get crabby."

"Bring the cow."

"You'd better be ready." Slim opened a sliding door and stepped outside. He removed the rope from the heifer's horns. "You ready?"

"Slim, I'm charging by the hour, so take as much time as you want."

Slim opened the trailer gate. The heifer came out like a cannonball and went charging into a crowding alley made of heavy pipe.

"Here she comes!"

CHAPTER ELEVEN

Big Trouble At the Vet Clinic

Doctor Skaggs was poised at the front of the squeeze chute, ready to close the head gate on her neck when she came through.

But then, at exactly the wrong time, the door into the office opened and out stepped Nikki, his secretary, a tall young lady with long brown hair. "Doctor, Nathan Dahlstrom called about his parrot and..."

Doc's attention strayed for just a second, and it was exactly the wrong second. The heifer blasted through the head gate, and, holy smokes, she was loose inside a closed area that contained four people and a dog! I can't speak for the people, but the dog was worried.

She was slipping and sliding on the wet

cement and had a wild look in her eyes. She snorted at Doc, then whipped her head around to Nikki in the door...and charged. Nikki uttered a scream and ducked into a supply closet.

This was BAD, but it got worse. The heifer went charging INTO THE WAITING ROOM, where people read magazines and wait for their doggies to get their shots and pills. By some struck of loke, the waiting room was empty.

Stroke of luck, it should be.

Slim and Doc looked at each other, I mean their gazes met like two swords clanging together. Slim said, "Aggie! Now what?"

A deadly silence fell over the place, as we all listened to the heifer rearranging the furniture in the waiting room. Doc said, "I'll go around and come in the front door."

"Yeah, and if she runs out the front door, we'll be chasing her down Main Street at midnight. I've got a better idea."

His gaze began creeping in my direction and it gave me the creeps. I edged closer to Miss Viola and, well, hid behind her legs. Maybe he would think I had gone for a walk or something. Vanished without a trace.

"Hank? Come here, boy, good dog."

I knew it! See, when they start the sweet talk

and the "good dog" stuff, it means trouble. I edged closer to Viola's warm legs and closed my eyes. Maybe if I pretended that I was back at the ranch, snapping at mosquitoes with Drover, it would all go away.

That happens in books, doesn't it? Sure it does, all the time. If you wish upon a star, the Teeth Fairy will come and, I don't know, leave a cookie or something.

I pressed my eyes shut and wished as hard as I could wish upon a star.

I felt a pair of hands upon me. I was being lifted off the cement floor. I opened my eyes and looked into the face of a scarecrow. Wait, it was Slim.

He wore an eerie smile. "Hankie, remember what I said back at the ranch?"

No.

"About being a hero and helping your friends?"

Oh, using me for bait? Forget that!

"Well, me and Doc have a little favor to ask. We sure could use some help."

I blistered him with a glare. I knew exactly what they were cooking up, and the answer was NO! I'd already had speaks with that heifer and she hated my guts. Furthermore, I had no wish to help a conniving cowboy and a vampire doctor. NO!

"Viola would be mighty proud."

Really? I turned my gaze around and searched the loveliness of her face. It was hard to read, but there was something in her eyes…

Okay, I would do it for Viola, and on the trip back home, if I lived that long, I would sit in her lap ALL THE WAY. Otherwise, no deal.

Slim held me pretty firmly in his arms, as though he thought I might try to escape. Okay, I did try to escape, but he was pretty stout in the arms and hands.

He walked to the open door that led into the office and reception area. We could hear odd noises inside. "Pooch, rush in there and give her a bark, then come on back. I think she'll take the bait."

There, you see? I knew it! Bait. These people have no shame, they'll ask their dogs to do anything.

"Bring her out and we'll trap her in the chute, then we can head for the house. Double dog food tonight, buddy."

Double dog food. Oh brother. If he ever tried to eat that stuff himself, he wouldn't give it as a prize, even to his worst enemy. Winning Double Dog Food was like two kicks in the tail instead of one.

Furthermore, brave dogs volunteer for dangerous jobs because it's RIGHT, not for the promise of Double Dog Food.

Okay, let's move on to the scary part.

It would have been fine if he had set me down just inside the door. That would have given me the option of, well, choosing my own manner of proceeding with this fiasco, but no, he didn't do it that way. He pitched me inside and yelled, "Go get 'er, Hankie! Send 'er to school!"

I went flying into the office area, landed on all-fours, and slid on Fully Extended claws across an expanse of slick limoleon floor. Mellonium. It was slick, and when I stopped sliding, I found myself...

Yipes, there she stood, eight hundred pounds of Malice with horns and a fever and a grudge against the world. She had knocked over two chairs and a coffee table and scattered magazines all over the place. She had also repainted the floor. Green.

Her eyes came at me like bullets...no, like artillery shells. She was panting and volcanic smoke rolled out of her nostrils. She lowered her head, shook her horns, and pawed up a couple of magazines.

Was there something I could say to, well, put her mind at ease and make her feel comfortable about being in Dr. Skaggs's waiting room? No. We had gone beyond that.

I took several short breaths of fresh carbon diego, then a big one, and launched into my presentation.

"Look at this mess! You ought to be ashamed of yourself. What would your mother think?"

She shook her horns and pawed up some more magazines. Her fuse was definitely lit and it was burning towards the dynamite. All she needed was one little nudge.

"Five bucks says you can't catch me." Then I

played the big card: I crossed my eyes and stuck out my tongue at her!

Wow, did that ever work! Here she came, the Midnight Express on a single-minded mission to run a horn right through my gizzard. We're talking about seriously angry and determined.

It wasn't easy for me to reach Escape Speed on that slick floor, but she didn't look so graceful either. I went sliding down the hall and she came sliding right behind me. I had a two-step lead and all I had to do was...

Wait, hold everything. Do you realize what would happen if THE DOOR BLEW SHUT? Don't forget, there was a breeze going through that hallway. You didn't think of that, right? Well, it's time for you to start thinking about it and to prepare yourself for...

Maybe we shouldn't go on with this.

Remember what we said about the children? Give 'em a few chills and goose bumps, but spare 'em from the really scary parts of my work. No kidding, I don't want to give 'em more than they can handle.

I mean, if that door blew shut, I would be trapped in the hall with no way out, trapped with an eight hundred-pound beast that wrecked dogs just for sport. And what if the door somehow locked and my so-called "friends" on the other side couldn't come to my rescue?

It would be bad. No, worse than that. It would be AWFUL—me locked inside the vet clinic with a heifer that had murder on her mind.

Those of us in Security Work have to come to grips with this stuff all the time, but what about the kids? What do you think? Do we dare go on?

I knew that's what you would say. Okay, have it your way, we'll risk it, but don't blame me if everything goes to blazes.

Ready?

There's one little detail I forgot to mention, heh heh. The door DIDN'T blow shut. I knew that and you didn't, but I just wanted to give you a little thrill. Hencely, at this point, everything looked good to go.

I went streaking down that hallway, shot through the door that hadn't blown shut, and headed straight for the nearest pair of legs to hide behind—Slim's. He was holding a gate made of iron pipe that led into the crowding pen, and he was poised to throw it shut when the heifer came through.

She came fogging out the door, looking around with wild eyes for something to hook and stomp. She saw Slim and made a run at him, but he was on the other side of a stout gate, so she snorted and kept hauling the mail. I stuck out my tongue at her as she blew past, and Slim swung the gate and fastened it with a piece of chain.

So far, so good. Our part was done and the cow was on her way toward the squeeze chute. Doc was waiting on the head gate, his expression as stiff as rawhide. He was determined not to miss the catch this time and get called an Aggie. The heifer clanged and banged toward the head gate, when all at once...

OH NO! Nikki appeared in the door, looking very pale, and said, "Is it over?"

I stopped breathing. So did Slim. Our respective gazes swung around to Doctor Skaggs. Would he...

The heifer saw daylight up ahead and plunged forward. There was a clang of steel and...he got her, by George! She was captured!

Doc wilted and grabbed a breath of air. Slim mopped his brow with a red bandana, then patted me on the ribs. "Nice work, pooch. And you too, Doc. Down in College Station, I'll bet the Aggie band is playing 'The Eyes of Texas.'"

Doc gave his head several shakes. "Slim, if the Aggie band ever played 'The Eyes of Texas,' the alumni association would shut down the school. Now, why don't you leave so I can get some work done. Tell Woodrow he can pick up the heifer day-after tomorrow."

Slim headed for the door but stopped to admire the diploma on the wall. "It's kind of amazing, what you can buy at a garage sale."

Doc threw a wet towel at him and we hurried out the door, with old Slim laughing his head off. What was so funny? I had no idea, but when you hang out with Slim, you get used to this kind of thing.

You're probably burning with curiosity, wondering what had happened to Miss Viola. Had she climbed up into the rafters or jumped into a storm cellar?

No, Slim had made her wait outside, just in case the heifer got loose again, and we found her waiting in the pickup. She was anxious to hear the whole story and I must admit that Slim gave a pretty accurate report. The main points were (you need to pay attention here) the main points were:

1. Hank volunteered for a very dangerous mission and performed in a heroic manner.
2. Down in College Station, the entire Aggie band was playing 'The Dogs of Texas."
3. Most likely, Hank would receive a huge T-bone steak as a reward.

There wasn't much I could add to that. Slim

had pretty muchly nailed it, and as you might expect, Miss Viola was extremely impressed. When we headed out of town, guess whose head was in her lap, and guess whose ears were being stroked.

Mine.

Slim had to drive and I could see that he was squirming with jealousy. Of course he couldn't resist making a smart remark. "You're going to ruin my dog. After all this pompering, he won't be worth eight eggs."

Miss Viola smiled. "The hero wins the lady. Sorry."

Slim got a laugh out of that, but she was exactly right. If you want to know who's the hero, he's the one with his head on the lady's lap, getting his ears rubbed.

But our day wasn't quite over. There was more.

CHAPTER TWELVE

Another Daring Rescue!

Well, the drive back to the ranch was just about perfect, until we came to that big hill where the highway drops down into the Wolf Creek valley. And there, we ran into what Slim had been worrying about all day: storm clouds, lightning and thunder, and sheets of rain.

See, whilst I had been fighting wild cows and saving ladies in distress, those fluffy Gulf clouds had clumped together and turned into big dark mountains that went way, way up in the sky, and they were full of thunder and lightning. The rain came hard and Slim had the windshield wipers flapping as hard as they would go.

By the time we reached the Wolf Creek road, it had become a muddy canal. Slim pulled over, unhooked the stock trailer, and left it parked on the side of the road, then locked the front hubs into four-wheel drive. By the time he dived back inside the cab, he was dripping water and had to wipe off his glasses.

We resumed our journey in Woodrow's clean pickup and we're talking about Serious Mud. I had to sit up and help with the driving. It had definitely become a four-wheel drive situation.

As we slipped and slode down the muddy road, Viola started singing in her sweet soprano voice. It was the kind of song they call "a round," which means it had two parts that fit together in harmony. It was a church song and Slim knew it, and he joined in and sang the second part.

It didn't have many words: "Dona nobis, pacem pacem." I had no idea what that meant, but it was a pretty song and a huge improvement over "Wet Boots."

So there we were in Woodrow's pickup, singing a pretty song and fish-tailing our way down five miles of muddy road, past ranch headquarters and on towards Viola's house. Rivers of water were rushing down both ditches and when we came to the low water crossing…fellers, the days of "low water" had come to an end. The creek was up, flooding across the road.

Slim stopped the pickup and studied the situation. "I don't think we'd better try to cross it. People get washed away in water like that."

Viola nodded. "I agree."

"But your daddy'll be pacing the floor. We'd better go back to headquarters and call, before he..." He narrowed his eyes. "Good honk, is that y'all's car?"

Viola looked and her eyes popped open. A car with headlights was coming toward us on the other side of the creek. "That's Mom's car. You don't suppose..." The cab fell silent. Everyone watched as the car kept coming.

Slim rolled down his window and waved his arm. The car kept creeping toward the foaming water. "It's Woodrow, and he's going to try to cross!"

"Oh my word!"

Slim chewed his lip and watched as the car's front tires entered the water. Deeper and deeper, until the water was over the hub caps. There, the car stopped.

Slim muttered, "The motor drownded out and we've got a problem. Does this pickup have a winch?"

"I think so, yes."

"You know how to run it?"

"No."

He studied the dash. "There's a switch over

here to the left of the steering wheel. 'In' and 'Out.' Start letting out the cable. When I reach him, I'll give the signal and you start spooling it back in." His gaze fell on me. I guess he noticed that I had gone into High Alert. "You stay here."

Yes sir.

He pushed open the door against the wind and stepped outside, and I dived out right behind him.

Well, what did he expect? When our people have to do rescues in deep water, they need a loyal dog to supervise and cheer them on. They don't always know that, but the dogs do, and sometimes we have to take matters into our own hands.

I heard him growl, "Disobedient whelp of a dog!"

Too bad. Could we get to work?

When we vacated the pickup, Viola scooted over to the driver's seat and started spooling out the winch cable. It had a metal hook on the end and Slim clipped it onto his belt. He waded into the rushing water. The current was so strong, it tried to sweep him downstream.

I went to the edge of the creek and started cranking out some Rescue Barks. "Keep moving! Don't let the current take you! Let's get that man out of the car, and hurry!"

This must have helped, because Slim kept slogging forward. By the time he reached the car, the water was above his knees. Fence posts and big tree limbs floated past, and holy smokes, a 30-gallon propane tank! Woodrow rolled down the window and I heard this exchanged.

Woodrow: "The darned thing quit on me."

Slim: "It drownded out."

"I'll get 'er started in a second."

"Forget the car. We need to get you out of here."

"Are you crazy? My wife'll shoot me if I leave her car in the creek!"

"Come on, get out."

"Go feather your own nest! I don't need any help!"

Slim grabbed the door handle and...this was hard to believe. Woodrow slapped down the door locker and yelled, "Why don't you mind your own business once in a while!"

"Woodrow, unlock the door or I'll bust out the window."

There was a long moment of silence, then... pretty scary, huh? You bet. Then Woodrow unlocked the door. Slim pulled on the door with all his might...but would he be able to get it open against the pressure of the water?

This was a critical moment in our rescue operation, so I dived into the water...yipes, it was frigid...I returned to dry land and doubled down on the Rescue Barks, I mean, we're talking about pumping out some BIG ONES.

Just what we needed! Slim got the door opened, pulled Woodrow out of the car, held on to him, and gave Viola the signal to start reeling in the cable. Heh. She did better than that. I guess she thought the winch was too slow, so she put the pickup in reverse, punched the gas, and hauled them back to dry land. I mean, she sledded 'em out of that water.

You talk about teamwork! Slim, Viola, and I had pulled off one of the most dramatic rescues of my entire career, and half an hour later, we were all sitting on Loper and Sally May's front porch, watching the rain come down.

Viola had called her mom and told her that everyone was fine but they would be stranded at Loper and Sally May's place until the creek went down.

Old Woodrow was decked out in Loper's bathrobe and sipping on a cup of hot chocolate, and he had become very quiet. I noticed that Viola had been speaking to him in a low, firm voice and all at once, he said, "You are the bossiest woman I ever met!"

On an ordinary day, Miss Viola was sweet, kind, and gentle, but at that moment, she gave him The Eye of the Cobra, stamped her foot, and said, "Daddy!"

He blinked, took a deep breath, and looked at Slim. "I'm sorry you got wet."

"His name is *Slim*."

Woodrow seemed to be in pain. "I'm sorry you got wet...Slim."

"And?"

"And...I guess I ought to thank you."

"For?"

"For bailing me out."

"Twice."

"Twice in one day."

Viola wilted, exhausted. "You are such a mess!"

Slim flashed a smile. "You're sure welcome, Woodrow, but we've got to give the credit to the real hero. Hank."

Did you hear that? Wow, I was astamished!

Okay, maybe he didn't say that, but he should have. I mean, nobody ever notices all the things dogs do behind the scenes, but...oh well, I ride for the brand and let others take all the credit.

The next day, they found the car. It got washed a hundred feet down the creek and came to rest against a cottonwood tree. It was a total loss and Woodrow was lucky he got out alive.

By the way, Rosella didn't murder him. In fact,

she was tickled pink with the way it turned out. She got a new car out of the deal and the insurance paid for most of it.

And that's all we can squeeze out of this story. Wait, one last thing. When the rain quit, I seized the opportunity to slip around to the iris patch

and caught Sally May's rotten little cat in a careless moment.

Hee hee. Just as the sun peeked out of the clouds and a big rainbow formed in front of the house, I ran Kitty up a tree and everything was right in the world.

It doesn't get any better than that, and this case is closed.

Have you read all
of Hank's adventures?

Finding Hank

The Most-Often Asked Questions
about Hank the Cowdog

For more than 35 years, John R. Erickson has entertained three generations of readers with Hank the Cowdog's hilarious antics, and now, for the first time, in this beautiful, full-color volume, he answers the most common questions he has received from fans over the years!

Written in an engaging question-and answer style, this collector's item — complete with illustrations and original photographs — provides a unique behind-the-scenes look at the people, places, and real-life animals and incidents behind your favorite Hank stories!

Coming Fall 2023

Read the short stories that started it all!

Believe it or not, once upon a time Hank the Cowdog was just *one* of many endearing characters who made their debut in an early collection of short-stories by beloved Texas author, John R. Erickson. First published under the title, *The Devil in Texas*, Erickson compiled his funniest fiction writings and released this book to his local ranching community. Inspired by the encouragement he received, he later developed one particular character, Hank the Cowdog, who quickly became a literary hero in his own right.

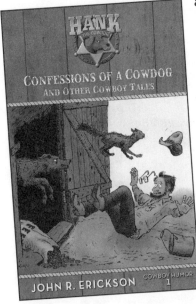

And, if you love Hank, you're in for a treat! In these stories, you'll get inside the head of an ornery bronc who's about to be saddle-broke, read the journal of a spunky ranch wife who has to find creative ways to get the cowboys to help her around the homestead, and gain some comical insights into what a cowboy's work really involves—the *unglamorous* side!

And, be sure to check out the **Audiobooks!**

If you've never heard a *Hank the Cowdog* audiobook, you're missing out on a lot of fun! Each Hank book has also been recorded as an unabridged audiobook for the whole family to enjoy!

Praise for the Hank Audiobooks:

"It's about time the Lone Star State stopped hogging Hank the Cowdog, the hilarious adventure series about a crime solving ranch dog. Ostensibly for children, the audio renditions by author John R. Erickson are sure to build a cult following among adults as well." — *Parade Magazine*

"Full of regional humor . . . vocals are suitably poignant and ridiculous. A wonderful yarn." — *Booklist*

"For the detectin' and protectin' exploits of the canine Mike Hammer, hang Hank's name right up there with those of other anthropomorphic greats...But there's no sentimentality in Hank: he's just plain more rip-roaring fun than the others. Hank's misadventures as head of ranch security on a spread somewhere in the Texas Panhandle are marvelous situation comedy." — *School Library Journal*

"Knee-slapping funny and gets kids reading."

— *Fort Worth Star Telegram*

Love Hank's
Hilarious Songs?

Hank the Cowdog's "Greatest Hits" albums bring together the music from the unabridged audiobooks you know and love! These wonderful collections of hilarious (and sometimes touching) songs are unmatched. Where else can you learn about coyote philosophy, buzzard lore, why your dog is protecting an old corncob, how bugs compare to hot dog buns, and much more!

And, be sure to visit Hank's "Music Page" on the official website to listen to some of the songs and download FREE Hank the Cowdog ringtones!

The Ranch Life Learning Series

Want to learn more about ranching? Check out Hank's hilarious and educational new series, Ranch Life Learning, brought to you by Maverick Books and The National Ranching Heritage Center!

Saddle up for some fun as the same cast of characters you've come to know and love in the Hank the Cowdog series gives you a first-class introduction to life on a ranch!

In these books, you'll learn things like: the difference between a ranch and a farm, how cows digest grass, what it takes to run a ranch as a successful business, how to take care of cattle throughout the various seasons, what the daily life of a working cowboy looks like, qualities to look for in a good horse, the many kinds of wild animals you might see if you spent a few days on Hank's ranch, the tremendous impact different kinds of weather have on every aspect of ranching, and, last but not least, the consequences and benefits of wildfires!

"Audio-Only" Stories

Ever wondered what those "Audio-Only" Stories in Hank's Official Store are all about?

The Audio-Only Stories are Hank the Cowdog adventures that have never been released as books. They are about half the length of a typical Hank book, and there are currently seven of them. They have run as serial stories in newspapers for years and are now available as audiobooks!

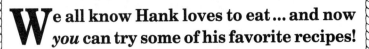

We all know Hank loves to eat ... and now *you* can try some of his favorite recipes!

Have you visited Sally May's Kitchen yet?

http://www.hankthecowdog.com/recipes

Here, you'll find recipes for:

Sally May's Apple Pie
Hank's Picante Sauce
Round-Up Green Beans
Little Alfred's and Baby Molly's Favorite Cookies
Cowboy Hamburgers with Gravy
Chicken-Ham Casserole
...and MORE!

Have you visited Hank's official website yet?

www.hankthecowdog.com

Don't miss out on exciting *Hank the Cowdog* games and activities, as well as up-to-date news about upcoming books in the series!

When you visit, you'll find:

- Hank's BLOG, which is the first place we announce upcoming books and new products!
- Hank's Official Shop, with tons of great *Hank the Cowdog* books, audiobooks, games, t-shirts, stuffed animals, mugs, bags, and more!
- Links to Hank's social media, whereby Hank sends out his "Cowdog Wisdom" to fans.
- A FREE, printable "Map of Hank's Ranch"!
- Hank's Music Page where you can listen to songs and even download FREE ringtones!
- A way to sign up for Hank's free email updates
- Sally May's "Ranch Roundup Recipes"!
- Printable & Colorable Greeting Cards for Holidays.

- Articles about Hank and author John R. Erickson in the news,

...AND MUCH, MUCH MORE!

BOOKS
The Collection

FAN ZONE
Fun & Games

AUTHOR
Meet the Creator

STORE
Books & More

Find Toys, Games, Books & More at the Hank shop.

ANNOUNCING:
A sneak peek at Hank #66

Ever thought of having a Hank the Cowdog Themed Party?

Hank Plays Cupid:

GAMES
COME PLAY WITH HANK & PALS

BOOKS
BROWSE THE ENTIRE HANK CATALOG

FRIENDS
GET TO KNOW THE RANCH GANG

 Visit Hank's Facebook page

 Follow Hank on Twitter

 Watch Hank on YouTube

 Follow Hank on Pinterest

 Send Hank an Email

FROM THE BLOG

JAN 26 Hank is Cupid in Disguise...

JAN 18 The Valentine's Day Robbery! - a Snippet from the Story

DEC 04 Getting SIGNED Hank the Cowdog books for Christmas!

OCT 14 Education Association's lists of recommended books?

VISIT THE BLOG

Hank's Survey
We'd love to know what you think!   GO

TEACHER'S CORNER

Download fun activity guides, discussion questions and more.

SALLY MAY'S RECIPES

 Discover delicious recipes from Sally May herself.   GO

Hank's Music. ♪
Free ringtones, music and more!

MORE

Official Shop
Find books, audio, toys and more!

LET'S GO

Join Hank's Security Force
Get the activity letter and other cool stuff.

JOIN   SECURITY FORCE

Get the Latest

Keep up with Hank's news and promotions by signing up for our e-news.

Looking for The Hank Time fan club newsletter?

Enter your email address

SIGN UP

Hank in the News

 Find out what the media is saying about Hank.

GO

FEATURED BOOK

The Christmas Turkey Disaster

Now Available!

Hank is in real trouble this time. L...

BUY   READ   LISTEN

BOOKS
Browse Titles
Buy Books
Audio Samples
Other Books

FAN ZONE
Games
Hank & Friends
Security Force
Educational Stuff

AUTHOR
John Erickson's Bio
Hank in the News
In Concert
Contact John

SHOP
The Books
Store
Get Help
Retailer Info

Teacher's Corner

Know a teacher who uses Hank in their classroom? You'll want to be sure they know about Hank's "Teacher's Corner"! Just click on the link on the homepage, and you'll find free teacher's aids, such as a printable map of Hank's ranch, a reading log, coloring pages, blog posts specifically for teachers and librarians, quizzes and much more!

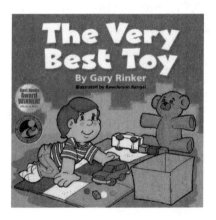

The following activities are samples from *The Hank Times*, the official newspaper of Hank's Security Force. Please do not write on these pages unless this is your book. And, even then, why not just find a scrap of paper?

"Photogenic" Memory Quiz

We all know that Hank has a "photogenic" memory—being aware of your surroundings is an important quality for a Head of Ranch Security. Now *you* can test your powers of observation.

How good is your memory? Look at the illustration on page 63 and try to remember as many things about it as possible. Then turn back to this page and see how many questions you can answer.

1. Was Hank's tail pointing UP or DOWN?

2. How many pickup tires could you see? 1,2,3, or 4?

3. Were there clouds in the sky?

4. Was Slim holding the door with HIS Left or Right hand?

5. How many of Hank's ears could you see? 1, 2, 3, or all 4?

"Word Maker"

Try making up to twenty words from the letters in the names below. Use as many letters as possible, however, don't just add an "s" to a word you've already listed in order to have it count as another. Try to make up entirely new words for each line!

Then, count the total number of letters used in all of the words you made, and see how well you did using the Security Force Rankings below!

DOCTOR   SKAGGS

_____	_____
_____	_____
_____	_____
_____	_____
_____	_____
_____	_____
_____	_____
_____	_____
_____	_____

56 - 59 You spend too much time with J.T. Cluck and the chickens.

60 - 63 You are showing some real Security Force potential.

64 - 67 You have earned a spot on our Ranch Security team.

68 + Wow! You rank up there as a top-of-the-line cowdog.

Yard Gate

The Yard Gate is a busy place on the ranch. Scrap Time is definitely one of Hank's favorite events. However, there are characters coming and going at all times at the yard gate. Let's go through the clues below and see if we can figure out in what order the characters below made an appearance at the Yard Gate. This may be our toughest puzzle ever. Good Luck!

Clues:

Drover was two spots before Hank
Snort's spot was double Pete's
Hank was in the middle

RIP
SNORT
HANK
DROVER
PETE

1. _____

2. _____

3. _____

4. _____

5. _____

"Rhyme Time"

If Dr. Skaggs were to leave Twitchell, what kinds of jobs do you think he could find? Make a rhyme using "Skaggs" that would relate to his new job possibilities.

Example: Doctor Skaggs runs a retirement spot
for old horses.

Answer: Skaggs **NAGS.**

1. Doctor Skaggs works in a store selling purses.

2. Doctor Skaggs makes conference name-badges.

3. Doctor Skaggs teaches dogs how to show that they're happy.

4. Doctor Skaggs prints monthly periodicals with articles about pets.

5. Doctor Skaggs waves these (yellow, checkered...) at car races.

6. Doctor Skaggs repairs bridges that are drooping a little.

7. Doctor Skaggs becomes a pro-team's spokesman, telling everyone how great the team is.

<u>Answers</u>:

1. Skaggs BAGS
2. Skaggs TAGS
3. Skaggs WAGS
4. Skaggs MAGS
5. Skaggs FLAGS
6. Skaggs SAGS
7. Skaggs BRAGS

John R. Erickson,

a former cowboy, has written numerous books for both children and adults and is best known for his acclaimed *Hank the Cowdog* series. The *Hank* series began as a self-publishing venture in Erickson's garage in 1982 and has endured to become one of the nation's most popular series for children and families.

Through the eyes of Hank the Cowdog, a smelly, smart-aleck Head of Ranch Security, Erickson gives readers a glimpse into daily life on a cattle ranch in the West Texas Panhandle. His stories have won a number of awards, including the Audie, Oppenheimer, Wrangler, and Lamplighter Awards, and have been translated into Spanish, Danish, Farsi, and Chinese. In 2019, Erickson was inducted into the Texas Literary Hall of Fame. *USA Today* calls the *Hank the Cowdog* books "the best family entertainment in years." Erickson lives and works on his ranch in Perryton, Texas, with his family.

Nicolette G. Earley

was born and raised in the Texas Hill Country. She began working for Maverick Books in 2008, editing, designing new Hank the Cowdog books, and working with the artist who had put faces on all the characters: Gerald Holmes. When Holmes died in 2019, she discovered that she could reproduce his drawing style and auditioned for the job. She made

her debut appearance in Book 75, illustrating new books in the series she read as a child. She and her husband, Keith, live in the Texas hill country.